I0877705

Wind in the Face

lisa glenn

PublishAmerica
Baltimore

First printing

All characters in this book are fictional and any resemblance to persons or activities are coincidental.

ISBN: 1-4137-1242-8
PUBLISHED BY PUBLISHAMERICA, LLLP
www.publishamerica.com
Baltimore

Dedication

This effort is dedicated to my Family
Randal, my anchor;
Brigit, Colleen, Kevin and Critter, my wind;
Chris, Ryan, and Brandon in "drydock";
To my parents Abilio & Virginia Martins,
Who always encouraged me to write a book;
To my grandparents who were always there for me,
now gone yet always with me;
Laudina & Regino Martins and Victoria & Benjamin
Donnelly;
And to my Aunt, Jean Fallin, who always listened;
To my brothers Michael and Stephen and their families,
…My sister Elaine, Over the Rainbow;
and to all my Martins, Moore, Vernon, Halloran and Glenn
Extended family;
As well as to all my sisters and brothers of the heart…
You know who you are!

Acknowledgments

Having at least half my roots originate in Portugal, a country along the sea and having spent a great many of my growing-up summers on the Chesapeake Bay, an affinity for the power and blessings of water comes naturally to me. Many have asked about me about my e-mail screen name and it recently it occurred to me that it indeed influenced the writing of this book…notes from the ark; and in the case of this story, e-mails among the main characters between the land and a boat! With that said…

Heartfelt thanks to a lifelong friend I've known since 7th grade, Nancy McCormick for helping me dive off and cheering me on; as well as for the buoys from another childhood (since kindergarten) friend, heart sister Chela Sullivan, and my mentor Carolyn Bowden for keeping me afloat as I chartered new waters. Even though my family and I have been transplant Texans for over twenty-three years, it was the Kelley family who opened my eyes to the hidden delights of Kemah and allowed my husband and myself to experience their forty-two foot Moody sailboat, 'Blue,' and the wonder of the holiday light show on the water. Jana Kelley, especially, I'd like to thank for all of her edits. Jana, along with Georgia McCalmon, were the first two friends, who are also inspiring teachers at Elkins High School, to read this completed 'work in progress' and who gave me invaluable feedback. They are both members of the Thunderbird Book Club to which I am honored to belong. To my daughter, Brigit, without whose help I would never have made the proof deadline, my deepest thanks and love.

While Alexandria, Virginia and the Washington, D.C. area will always call me back to the place where I grew up and to my core network from there (the Beckmans, Berrys, Bystrans, Cilinskis,

.

DeGiorgis, Feeney-Coyles, Mr. Curran, Foleys, Lauxes, Montgomerys, Riesgos and Sullivans), Texas has given me so many women friends of true grit and style....Kay McConaughey (for her spirit, her flamingos, and gifting me the once in a lifetime experience of meeting Robert Harling, who wrote *Steel Magnolias*), Margie (and the Wilde ones), Glenda, Sally, Kath, Susan, Lee, Debbie, Rox, Arleen, Sandy, Franny, Chel, Amy, Barbara, Victoria, Donna, Beth...While men may be the ones 'we can't live without,' it is our sisters of the heart who sustain us in Faith through all times. It is a composite of these real life characters, both male and female, which are just as much a part of me as my birth DNA, that gave life to the pages within. Each character is truly a fictional composition of many parts and many hearts!

A special thanks to Bob Haenel, Editor of the *Herald Coaster*, and Bev Carter, owner of the *Southwest Star*, who let me hone my writing skills in their newspapers and to all my boys and co-workers at *Legacy* and *Leonetti Graphics* who there are no words to describe!

Finally, to those who fought the good fight against cancer along with my sister Elaine, yet have crossed over and are now our Guardian Angels...Karen Kelly O'Neill, Brigid Sullivan Healey, Mary Engelman, and Dallas Camp Temple.

Airplane Peanuts

Thirty-Five years of friendship was their legacy—thirty-five years!!!! Laughing to herself, Magdalina could easily recall when she and Tia had thought that at the sophisticated age of thirty-five they'd have it all. Now that chronological number seemed like midlife teens! Of course, spiced between these 'grownup' years were some fun wine-time lunches down by the Potomac, when Magdalina traveled back East, quick in-person catch-ups, between phone calls, e-mails and cards.

Magdalina was both anxious and excited about the upcoming visit; wondering what it was going to be like to spend an entire week with Tia again. She was apprehensive (to say the least) about whether this longtime friend would really be able to accept the low-key life she so prized. No one called her Lina except for Tia—"With that name, it sounds like I should be doing a rosary in your honor," Tia had quipped to Magdalina when they first met. This plunge into togetherness after so long would either prove soul sisters couldn't be separated at the hip or they'd each go off running in opposite directions in the dervish of yet another midlife crisis.

Since *September Eleventh*, meeting a friend at the airport took on new meaning. Lina had flown several times to visit family; this was the first time since the brutal attack on America for Tia. In the past few years Tia had begun to embrace traveling by air as almost spiritual. Since the devastating attack on New York City, one of the most exciting cities she had ever visited, Tia didn't feel within herself the trust needed to believe a person could even survive something simple much less a sky ride. Lina knew Tia wasn't alone in that feeling. The entire country seemed to carry the scars from that day on their hearts.

Above the clouds, Tia was thinking she could sure use the glass of chilled wine she knew Lina would have waiting for her. However, unlike Lina who liked to lose herself on her laptop or within the pages of a book in flight, Tia preferred to keep her wits about her when suspended thousands of miles above solid ground.

Magdalina's husband, Rod, dropped her at baggage while he circled the passenger pickup area. With all the heightened airport security, only those flying or having flown, were allowed in the gate areas.

Weaving her way through the maze of people and suitcases, Magdalina found her way over to the carousel where Tia's flight baggage was coming down…and there stood her lil' powerhouse of a friend. Tia was planted right next to the merry-go-round of luggage, oblivious to everything except watching for her bag. Magdalina knew it would be a big one because Tia, even though she said she had a gypsy spirit, wasn't a light packer. More excited to see Tia than she anticipated, Magdalina snuck up beside her with an exuberant "Hi." And so it began…again…

Razzleberry Pie

Arriving at Lina and Rod's home in the flat Houston 'burbs, Tia's suitcase was deposited in the guest room Lina had so carefully prepared. She had even set up the small TV-VCR unit they had once used on long car trips with the kids, for the late-night Tia, who Magdalina knew was still an ole' movie addict. Not bothering to unpack, Tia made her way back to the kitchen. Around the kitchen island, they nestled with slices of razzleberry pie, a tongue-tingling food sensation Tia's pallet hadn't experienced up until now, a veritable food orgasm! The hot tub beckoned; and the two were off to deflate and celebrate their right to be together, laughing, teasing and wanting to savor the moment.

Reunited with the precious commodity of quality time, they were both a bit pensive about what to expect even though they would demand little of the other. Lina did know one thing. She did not want to be placed in the role of 'bone in the middle,' listening to Tia share the details of her tight-wire relationship with Rory. Lina had known Tia since grade school, Rory since high school. Magdalina, admittedly was somewhat more protective of him. Why? It was probably the caretaker within; Rory appeared more passive and Tia, well, Tia gave the phrase, "the force be with you" new meaning!

Lina did understand deep down under the surface more than Tia credited her with. No one's marriage was easy. In doing research for her wide array of columns, Lina found it interesting that not many mammals or even birds mated for life! She herself had ripped the fabric of her own life over fourteen years ago, even though it took her almost seven years to make the decision. Walking away from her marriage with her children to start completely over was the most painful journey she had ever undertaken. It had been the right decision for her and in the long term even for her children; yet she knew that it's only in looking back that we have the clarity of 20/20 vision.

Ironically, Tia was one of the few people at that juncture who had understood and had been somewhat of a personal cheerleader for her. Lina's parents, though they had never been really comfortable with her 'Texas ex,' thought him a wonderful provider. Products of the post-war years, they had a tough time grappling with Lina's choice to leave behind the stay-at-home mommy world in which she excelled to become an exhausted working-mother with not enough hours in the day.

Taught her entire life by the good Franciscan sisters, and having a Catholic school May-Queen mentality, Lina had certainly felt like the woman wearing the scarlet letter after her divorce. Two factors at that time had been the catalyst she needed...her dying friend, Helena, with the message that life is too short and too precious. The other and maybe more powerful was her then passion for a love of long ago, the proverbial brass ring. Lina learned you *could* have it all...just not all at the same time.

She loved both Tia and Rory. They were thicker-than-blood friends. When she checked her e-mail each morning before starting her column, there was almost always one awaiting her from Rory...sometimes a colorful graphic that would make her smile, sometimes a plea for a kick-in-the-butt jump-start to get him and his day off the dime...it was never more than a few lines. Lina knew no one that worked harder for his family than Rory...two jobs, up before daybreak each morning. He was a gentle soul who had trouble facing his own ghosts at times. He wasn't a detail person; he wasn't perfect. Who was? Tia on the other hand was a passionate flame, literally the kind of friend who would do ANYTHING for you. Lina laughed remembering the time Tia had express mailed her favorite cookies from Brenners Bakery back in Virginia to her for her birthday. Tia had wrapped each one individually in wax paper. Always the type to make the time to listen, to be there for you...hang the dusting or the laundry...they could wait. With Tia, her children, her family and those blessed to be loved by her knew they were at the top of any mental to-do list she might have. Tia was also the ultimate lioness where her children were concerned, with which Lina could totally relate, always calling herself a mama bird.

Tia and Lina, two strong women, soul-bound sisters crusading for the children of the world...todays and tomorrow's...Lina through her writing and Tia through a local advocacy program. Lina had found her way through the mists, and though she still got lost from time to time, knew that if she couldn't save herself, she wouldn't be able to save anyone else. Now it was Tia's turn...

Red or White?

Hard on herself, Tia had always been a bit of a self-analyst who certainly knew right from wrong. Like many of her friends from childhood Tia was also someone who thought outside of the box, having somewhat of a cosmic belief system that all manner of stimuli could and would enter one's life to create change. An Eve of sorts, was it so wrong to drink from the fountain when the water tasted so good? Through Tia's gazing ball, nothing was permanent and everything could be a valid learning experience.

The self-assured Tia of today was a far cry from the adolescent Lina had known in grade school. It was in Lina's home, not her own, that Tia learned her first lesson in survival. Many of Lina's friends had been close to her mom, and Lina's house was the one on the block where they all tended to gather. Her mom made them feel more grownup because she talked to them in her tell-it-like it-is no-nonsense manner. Many times Lina had felt her mom was too blunt and graphic. Yet her adamant tirades seemed to get through to most, if not everyone. Protecting her close-knit family, Tia kept a great deal of herself locked away and only wished Lina's mom had seen fit to set her straight when Rory came along. Even with growing maturity, Tia had latched on to Rory like barnacles to a sunken vessel. Maybe it was the drama queen within her, yet all those decades ago Tia truly believed she had to have Rory to survive. She never really tricked him, yet always found a way back to his side after breakups and separations. Born on the cusp of women's lib, the outspoken Tia of today was back then quite simply under the misguided illusion that life was just not worth living if she had to live it without Rory. She was not the only female out there who thought that way...unbelievably, there was an entire generation of women who thought a man was needed for a woman to be complete.

For some time now, Tia had been trying to figure out how to validate her path…how to deal with the 'ripples' of her stone skipped across the water…

"Would you believe? A full moon just for us!" Tia laughed as she eased herself into the steaming water. She was supposed to be the free spirit in this duo yet she was the one donning a swimsuit.

"Red or White?" asked Lina with a bottle of each and two patio plastic wine glasses in her hand that she set on the edge of the decking.

"White and I hope it's really cold," retorted Tia.

"Do you want some water first?" asked Lina?

"No, just give me the good stuff…NOW!!" Tia chuckled.

"What's with the pink flamingo?" Tia questioned, nodding toward the bright metal flamingo in the terra cotta planter nearby.

"I've always been drawn to their quirky shape and bright color," responded Lina. "Also, a good friend from my ole' book group who moved away was really into them…she's my Texas Tornado who at sixty-something plus is trying new things all the time. She has a group of friends that 'flock' together once a year for some hair-raising adventures. Because of their color, several of the breast cancer fund-raising groups that I've written pieces on use them as their symbol, and I've also come to find a lot of unique women use them as their totem. In fact the two women who run our city's media department have them flying here and there all over their control room." Lina paused for a second to study her flamingo before adding, "I know when I observe one in someone's personal space, I inwardly perk to that person's energy. My dad has used that one you see in the planter as a pattern and has cut several out of wood for me that I've painted for friends."

Lina poured the wine, handed a glass to her friend, set her own down, and then untied the robe, submerging her birthday-suited self into the water with her glass held high above her head. Heaven-forbid any scented tub water mixed with the vino!

Tia raised her glass towards Lina's…"Here's to us! To a GREAT

WEEK!"

"To US and a GREAT week," mirrored Lina.

Tia sighed in blissful content. It was like she was in another world…away from the kids, Rory, her problematic reality. "Lina, no matter how much you miss the East, I just don't know why you would ever contemplate moving from this place, this view…" Even with just the light from the moon, the willow tree at the water's edge was reflected in the pond's stillness…there were even a couple of wild birds perched on the limbs…

"Are you ready to turn fifty?" Tia had already jumped into the dreaded decade debacle and wanted to know how Lina was dealing with the half-century mark approaching.

"Ready or not it's going to happen. I keep telling Rod I want a facelift or tummy tuck for the momentous moment event, though I keep replaying the fact that Paolo at my office guessed my age as thirty-eight! My ego wants to believe he meant it yet I know he was probably just sucking up."

Tia quipped back, "That would be cheating!!!! I know what you mean though…I'm determined to look damn good for my second time around. And I refuse to let my boobs blend into my tummy! I could still lose a good fifteen pounds."

Shifting in the steam both reached for their wine. "Second time around?" Lina asked, "Are you about to tell me you are going to fall in love again and remarry?"

"You don't have to remarry or fall in love, kiddo. You only have to believe the second chance is right around the corner. Maybe I will become a transplant here with you. Have you ever heard of a free pass?"

"Free pass?" questioned Lina, "I didn't know free passes existed. You really have been watching too much Disney, Tia"

"Come on," urged Tia, "Open up that writer's imagination you're supposed to have…it's when you imagine your life was changed through no fault of your own. You didn't make the decision to get a divorce; you didn't just pack up and leave—yet, one day, poof, everyone who needs you is not there, and you get to begin all over again."

Contrary to what she had told herself, Magdalina didn't want to get into it during this week with Tia, Lina knew, with every cell in her Sagittarian psyche, that this was the time to clear the air between them. She was just nervous on how to begin. Tia, like Lina's own mother, (now gone from this earth, yet forever present in some way) had always intimidated her by the sheer power she put behind her words whether talking about preschools or politics…and Lina knew Tia was not going to want to hear what she had to say.

"Whaaaaatttt??????" Tia questioned in an exacerbated tone.

"Damn! You still read my mind," Lina breathed out…"More Wine?!"

"You won't get any argument from me," said Tia, "I'm on vacation."

Lina refilled their glasses…breathed deeply, exhaled and then dove into friendship's deep waters.

"Tia, I know you think I don't understand your world; that you think I'm more in Rory's corner than yours, yadayadayadayada…You're wrong! I understand more than you realize…I feel your frustration and his. You think I think he's the only victim. In some ways, each of you, including those beautiful children of yours are victims. Sometimes I realize you feel negative vibes from me. What you're picking up on, though, is not a lack of empathy or understanding. It's simply my gut reaction or my backing off from all that anger you emit. And of course, you're angry…angry at Rory's family, the ones who didn't give him the love that you give anyone you love with every fiber of your being. You're angry at him—yet most of all, my friend; I think you are very angry at yourself and who you were back when you decided he was IT."

Before Tia could interject, Lina's hand shot out, ramrod straight, in the policeman's stop position. "No, don't say anything YET…let me get this out. This has been the dark cloud in our relationship; the ugly underbelly we're both afraid to rupture. You may have been the one who, as our mothers used to say, 'chased Rory till he caught you.' You may have even leapt from one bad decision to another because you felt trapped; however, you did NOT enter the relationship alone…you may feel like the responsible one; yet you are not the only one responsible. There I've said it."

"Okay, Lina, I'll think about it."

"Hell, lightning didn't even strike! Really, Tia, I think if you could just forgive the girl inside who made the mistakes, the woman you are would find a solution."

Tia pulled herself out of the steam to cool off…she had no words to give back because part of Lina's armchair psychology actually made sense for once.

Feeling comfortable with the silence, pulling on her robe around her bare skin, Lina said "Wish we had a Swischer Sweet to top off this evening."

"You don't smoke," retorted Tia, "and neither do I."

"Yeah, I know, yet those thin baby cigars just mellow out a moment every once in awhile," said Lina.

"You are still an idealist, Lina, if you think a lil' cigar can mellow out THIS moment! Let's get some sleep. You're up waaaaaaay past your bedtime and it's time, I think, to let our dreams take the night over."

Shorts, Slacks, or Crab Cakes?

The week had gone by all too quickly…unbelievably neither Tia or Lina had felt the need to dissect that first night's conversation in the hot tub or Lina's incredibly insightful take on Tia's situation. In fact, Tia had to admit that this week Lina had not only fed her bodily incredibly good soul food, Lina had also given her food for thought as well as the time to digest it at her own pace. It was and unexpected gift she truly appreciated.

Having quality one to one time with Rod yesterday had been an unexpected treat for Tia. Lina had a deadline job and Friday being Rod's afternoon off, he offered to take her to a historical yet real working western ranch off the Brazos. During her Lone Star week, she hadn't really done much shopping so at the ranch's unique little gift shop, she had indulged. She'd bought Rory a Texas a handcrafted metal Texas Flag he could hang on the back patio, her son, Sam, a hat, and her daughter, Meg, a real Texas bandana she could wear to keep her hair back while she crewed. At lunch they'd even eaten off a chuck wagon which had to explain why the baked beans tasted so good…or was it the mesquite wood they were cooked over that enhanced that intangible flavor.

Tia couldn't believe it was the last full day of her visit. Each one had flown by and she felt soooo good. Each morning she had worked out, run on Lina and Rod's treadmill to Lina's golden oldies CDs. She'd even had an apple a day (what could be healthier than that!)! Despite all the dining out they had done during the week, she felt good about her body and herself. The weather had even cooperated. Lina had told her that February in the southwest Houston 'burbs could be very iffy…yet the sun had shown just for her this week. Unlike their mutual friend, Gracie, who had battled and survived cancer twice back home, and who covered herself completely, like Katherine Hepburn in African Queen, Tia had taken every advantage of just vegging out back by the pool. She roasted her olive skin, decadently slathered in baby oil, allowing it to be exposed to the first hot rays that teased of a sensuous springtime. Back home, still shivering, everyone was going to be jealous of her Texas tan. "I'm not going to let myself think about the flight back. As Scarlet says, "that's for tomorrow," Tia lectured herself. She was really looking forward to this trip to Kemah near Galveston Bay.

Knowing how much Tia was drawn to the Native American culture, Lina had given her a bit of pre-trip trivia last night telling her that Kemah was an Indian word meaning 'wind in the face.' With an inner smile, she recalled the time she and Lina had ridden horses on the beach in Galveston a few years back on a previous visit. A fantasy ride every few years wasn't a lot to ask, was it?

"Ready to go, ladies?" Rod had the keys in his hand, his digital camera hanging on his shoulders.

Lina, in leggings and a bright yellow fleece looked over at Tia in her shorts, tank and hooded sweatshirt and said, "You're going to freeze your butt off down there by the water."

"No, I'm not," said Tia, "In the sun it'll be warm."

…And Tia was right. The sky was picture perfect blue, the breeze brisk, the sun shimmering, and they were feeling its kiss as they sat at the corner picnic table on the outside patio of Joe's Crabshack. It couldn't get much better than this. Lina was sipping a frosty fruit concoction while Rod and Tia were nursing Coronas feasting their wintered eyes on a parade of vessels passing by…even if they were just onlookers, it was simply fun reading the names on the sterns…Blue, Cancer-Free, Misty Lady, Gone Crazy…

Wind-whipped hair, focused weekend corporate captains at the wheel, lazy ladies armed with books and sunscreen, life-jacketed youngsters bouncing with excitement, toned twenty-somethings showing off their weekday workouts, Texas tough hotties doing the same…it was literally a bevy of boaters happy to be out on the Gulf this beautiful day in the tease of Spring, despite the slight nip in the air.

Awaiting the burger Lina had been craving, Rod's gumbo and her own crab cake lunch, Tia was thinking, "I could sit here forever."

Splat!!!!!

"Gross," muttered Tia.

"This is a first! I can't tell you how many times I've had lunch or dinner along this boardwalk and I've never EVER seen someone actually hit by gull droppings before. It's supposed to be a sign of good luck," laughed Lina. "Really...I forgot who told me yet I distinctly remember it because, c'mon who would associate bird splat with good luck normally??!!!"

"You and your birds," Tia said shaking her head with a good sport smile. "Despite the risk of bad karma, I think I'll just go wipe off this piece of lady luck-yuck before our meal arrives."

Gull seasoning forgotten, the three friends were once again comfortable just enjoying their leisurely lunch, enhanced by the salty air...table talk was irrelevant as they each wrapped themselves in their own blanket of thoughts.

Tia, gazing out over the deck, suddenly ejected, "This is impossible!"

Lina tried to take in where Tia was staring. It had been more than a long time since she had heard this particular inflection in her friend's voice. It was shocked surprise laced with excitement?! Being a writer, Lina found herself always searching for words to describe moods and moments.

All Lina could see was a man with dark hair, salted at the edges with white like a Margarita glass, attractive, yet sitting alone, looking out at the water nursing a cool drink, just as they had been. He looked vaguely familiar though she really could not place him.

"Who do you think that is?" Lina asked, as she noticed Tia making a move. "You aren't going over there are you? You really think you know him? You don't know anyone down here except us."

Tia stood up, "I've made a fool of myself before. This won't be the last time. I will be right back."

Shaking her head with a Mona Lisa smile, Lina watched her

friend. Through all this, Rod had been oblivious at the other end of the deck snapping pictures. Lina held her breath for her friend. "Hopefully, we'll have a good laugh over this later."

Lina was now the one staring. "Oh, my G…" This man did know Tia. He appeared surprised to see her, too, and to Lina's astonishment, he seemed to be asking Tia to sit down. To think, she had actually been smirking to herself that they had gotten through an entire week without any major trouble. Now here it was at the week's end with a giant exclamation point. Yet, for some reason, watching Tia's radiant face, Lina felt fifteen again.

Oysters Anyone?

"Rod, we can't just stand up here forever pretending to take pictures!"

"Who's pretending and anyway, why not?" Rod chuckled, "You're just dying to know what's going on down there?"

"Well, if the shoe were on the other foot, wouldn't you be?"

"Tia will call us over when she's ready," laughed Rod.

"Or not," quipped Lina, thinking Rod was the most infuriatingly patient man she'd ever met...it was what she loved most about him and what drove her absolutely crazy!!!!! *We could turn into Texas toast*, she thought, 'before Tia shares a bite of that one.' The guy was not movie star material yet was easy on the eyes, that's for sure...not too tall and fit, oh yeah...he was what you'd call 'catch of the day.'

As in times past, it seemed her brain barely finished a thought, when Tia's picked it up. There was Tia motioning them over to the lower deck of the restaurant next door where she and the mystery man were sitting. Lina and Rod made their way down the stairs and crossed the deck to where Tia and the stranger were waiting.

"Lina, Rod, this is Gabe Gibonni. He's visiting Texas, too, for a bit of R and R as well as golf." Niceties (as well as questioning looks between the friends) were exchanged. Lina and Rod sat down with Lina's mind working overtime to bring back the name Gibonni from the past.

She didn't have to work long...

"Lina, Gabe is the one who used to live in that apartment below us; one of those stand-up guys who has worked for the Bureau for years. He's actually looking at some property down here so he can golf all year round when he retires. He just asked if we'd like to join him for dinner later."

"Gabe, that's very generous of you. Rod and I have to get back, though, as my son's home for the weekend from college and being the hover-mother I am, I know that if I don't catch him at mealtime, I won't catch him at all. When the sun goes down, he and his ole high school buddies that are back in town for the weekend leave the nest with partttteeey plans on the brain."

"No problem. Another time…though I hope you'll let me borrow Tia for the evening. Though we just discovered we still live in the same city, we haven't seen each other in years, and I'd really enjoy the opportunity to catch up."

Before Lina could reply or offer an excuse, Tia said, "Oh, they won't care. They've been stuck with me all week and are probably ready for a quiet night. Gabe, do you have wheels to get me back? My flight is early tomorrow morning."

"As a matter of fact, I did rent wheels for the week…it's a Jeep, Tia, so it may not be the smoothest of rides."

Laughing and never one to let a line pass her by, Tia said, "My life could use a few humps and bumps!"

With that, Lina almost choked. Rod gently took his wife's arm and began diplomatically leading her away, "Honey, let's go get you some water. Gabe, nice to meet you. Tia, see you later."

Coffee-Black!

Even though she had fallen asleep very very late or very early, whatever way you viewed the sun coming up, Lina, arose with the birds as usual...and where in the hell was Tia?? She could just wring her neck...in just two hours they needed to leave for the airport if she was going to catch her flight back. Who knows, maybe she meant to miss the damn flight. "Why should I care?" Lina thought to herself..." though I'm going to be the one that has to call Rory and say, "Hey buddy, you don't have to be at National at 2:45...your wife? Well, I'm not sure where she is!"

She hoped Rod would keep on sleeping as she sipped her coffee and looked out at the lake...it's view wasn't bringing her any peace this morning.

There. She distinctly heard a door slam...and she had left the door unlocked...despite her doubts about Tia, she did have faith that she'd return if only for her kids' sake.

"Don't...Don't you dare look at me like Mother Superior," Tia's eyes flashed, despite her intense whisper. "Don't say a word. Not a single word. You are my dearest friend, yet I'm not going to allow even you to ruin the last 24 hours with some reality guilt trip. Just leave me alone, please. I'm going upstairs to shower and pack. Yesterday, Rod suggested that he take me to the airport so you could get Brady back off to college, and I think it's better that way."

Lina handed her a cup of coffee and turned around, barely concealing the confusion and hurt she felt.

Dreamcicles

Tia had known Lina was going to be worried. It was a not a typical parting for the two of them. Goodbye was not really in their vocabulary to one another anyway.

Tia was home. Her children had survived, and Rory was calm because without her around, he had made no mistakes... any that she could trace YET.

Now that everyone was off to work and school, Tia sat at the computer, knowing she needed to begin the reconnection with Lina across the miles via their regular modus operandi, e-mail. Usually she wrote to Lina's at her linesbylina column address (with her ee cummings lower case "l.") Tia wondered if Lina realized there were generations ahead of them and generations succeeding them who didn't evenknow who ee cummings was! Lina signed on to that handle each weekday morning and didn't sign off till dinner time. In a way, their weekly, sometimes daily e-mails, created a journal of their lives. It was less expensive and more therapeutic than the telephone yet sometimes they needed that "voice" connection too.

Tia signed on and she should have known, there was an e-mail from Lina waiting.

Subj: Miss you Already
Date: 2/24/02
To: Tiara
From: linesbylina

Tia,
 The house is so quiet...Brady just took off down the road back to school and Rod is probably on his way home from

dropping you at the airport. Inside, I feel so empty...this big kid-less house has really been an adjustment. Losing my mom right on the heels of Brady leaving for college might have magnified what I am feeling or whatever it is I am going through. I don't know. Anyway, having you here was just such fun...and I'm sorry the visit ended on such a tense note. I'll admit I was worried when you did not come home by the witching hour AND about what I'd say to Rory if he called or you were going to miss the flight altogether. You were probably right to warn me to keep my big Sagittarian mouth shut when you walked in or I might have said something we'd both regret.

You know I love you and am ready to listen when you're ready to share.

Love,
me

Subj: Truce!
Date: 2-26-02
From: Tiara
To: linesbylina

Okay, I know what you're probably thinking. Nothing happened!

Flashback first...Almost immediately after Rory and I got married I realized what a gigantic step I'd taken. To say I was in shock was an understatement...and I couldn't admit to even you that I might have made a mistake. I felt like a fool for being so quick to jump into the marriage market. Gabe would come up the walk at night and sometimes we'd just have a beer on the apartment steps and yack about our days. I was really drawn to him, yet being the good Catholic girl I'd been raised to be, I knew there was no looking back. So I moved on. When we bumped into one another in Kemah I just had to seize the moment. Carpe Diem as they say...

Subj: Really?
Date: 2-27-02
From: linesbylina
To: Tiara

You spent from 2:00 p.m. Saturday afternoon till 6:00 a.m. Sunday morning and you just talked. Care to share?

Subject: Really!!!!
Date: 2-28-02
From: Tiara
To: linesbylina

Sure.....
Gabe simply seemed glad to see someone he knew...that's it. When he asked if I wanted to join him for dinner that day, it just seemed like a 'gift' that I could not give up. Then after you and Rod left, we toured the entire Kemah Boardwalk...all those shops, listened to the Western singers... watching the kids hop in and out of that crazy star dancing fountain, where you never know when the water will shoot up!!!! I even tried it and got soaked, of course!! We had dinner at your favorite place, Willie G's, (sorry I didn't eat Chicken Rockefeller in your honor—you know I had to have the seafood platter) then walked over to the marina, wandering up and down between the boat slips wondering at all the unusual names. Gabe even took me on board this beautiful 42 foot Moody that belongs to a friend of his, that was like a work of art with its clean sleek lines. Please believe me and TRY TO UNDERSTAND.

Love,
 me
P.S. You're the one who told me that seagull splat was good luck!!!!

Higher than a kite could fly...oh baby did I feel HIGH!

"Dusting be damned," Tia thought to her self as she got up from the computer and headed toward the microwave to zap a cuppa tea. It was cold outside yet she would give herself a few minutes while the house was quiet to indulge in some of the recalled Texas heat of last week. In some ways it felt like yesterday and in other ways it seemed already too long ago. Except for Sam and Meg, she'd much rather be there than here. The grass is always greener...she exhaled on a sigh.

Walking with the aroma of the cinnamon tea towards her favorite chair, she sunk into is secure embrace, sipped, and then closed her eyes and allowed herself to feel the sunshine caressing her body on Lina's back deck or even the glow she felt after running on their treadmill in a mindless rock-out run. Yes, she could even feel the remembered rays of the Kemah Boardwalk as she and Gabe stopped here and there amidst the carnival like atmosphere. Best of all was riding the Ferris Wheel, gazing out over the bay and wishing she could stay that high forever...

Subj: Pandora's Box
Date: 3-1-02
From: linesbylina
To: Tiara

Oh, Tia... The other day when we were in Kemah and you catapulted down to check out this stranger on the lower deck at that place (what was it) between Joe's and the Flying Dutchman, I was watching your spontaneity, feeling like we were 15 again. We're not though! We've both learned that even though fate moves us around at times like pieces on a chessboard, we ultimately have to make the choice on the next move.

And, of course I understand!!!!!! Remember, I've been there, done that 'gift to yourself' routine. I've experienced that meant-to-be/he's-the-one connection. Do I believe in magic? Yes. Do I believe it lasts beyond all else? No! I learned the hard way—Some times love is truly just not enough, cliché and all. The gift moment turns into a night, the night into clandestine afternoons, and obsessively grabbed time where-ever, whenever you can find it. Do I have regrets? Hell, yes! Lost time and focus on my children during their most precious years being the biggest. Would I jump off that same cliff again? Probably...that free fall woke me up and showed me I had it in me to make the choices I needed to make. Do I want to see anyone I love take that kind of risk for the return? Honestly, I just don't know...
Getting off my soapbox...

Love,
me

Subj: Dreamsicle
Date: 3-02-02 10:00 p.m.
From: Tiara
To: linesbylina

Lina, the place was 'Cadillac Bar' (you know me first class ride all the way despite my propensity for VW Beetles vs. luxury cars)...Girlfriend, you don't have to warn me. Only too well do I remember your own trial by fire; yet like a precious metal fired, you emerged from your shaman desert a stronger brighter more independent being. Unfortunately, my rendezvous with Gabe is probably going to remain just what it was...a Margarita Dreamsicle! You know how when you crave something so bad you can smell it, feel it, taste it, even though it's not in your hand?!!!! No matter what else, I'm determined I'm going to lose that weight I've been hoping to shed and fill myself with Margarita Dreamsicles instead.

    Gotta run...Meg needs to get to her painting class and I need to stop and pick up Sam from school. Thanks for being there.

Love,
me

Subj: Back to Normal
Date: 3/5/02 5:00 a.m.
From:Ror7
To: linesbylina

    Hey Girl! What'd you do to my wife? Ever since she got back from her visit with you, she's been a bundle of energy...cleaning, reorganizing. I kinda like it...yet whaaazzzz up??? She also told me she ran into our old neighbor Gabe...can you believe? Trite but true...what a small world!

Subj: Contagious Cleaning
Date: 3/6/02 6:30 a.m.
From: linesbylina
To: Ror7

    Hey yourself! Was wondering when you were going to e-mail me again.

    Remember the sign you and Tia gave me for my birthday one year that said, 'Blessed are they who clean up.' Well, I think she liked our everything-in-its place house. What you both have to remember though, is that even though I've always been a neat-knic, there are now no kids around to mess up! Looking back now I wonder how ever accomplished what I did in the hours allotted to one day...guess that's why I was a wee bit thinner then!

Subj: Check'n IN
Date: 3/17/02
To: Tiara
From: Gabewing

Tia, I should have at least tried to call when I got back to town to thank you for having dinner with me in Kemah and to make sure you made it back on time for your flight. It wasn't my initial intent to keep you out all night when we bumped into one another in Texas of all places.

You still appear to be the 'lil fireball you were years ago and I'm just sorry that you and Rory seem to be caught between a rock and a hard place in your marriage. Maybe that's why I've never taken the plunge...too chicken to take a risk. Hey, I finally figured out your e-mail handle...Tiara...since you're not the prissy princess type, it's got to mean Queen of everything, right?

Happy St. Patty's Day to you and yours,
Gabe
P.S. You should stop feeling so self-conscious about your weight...a lot of men like their women 'Rubenesque.'

Subj:Dreamsicles
Date: 3/18/02
To: linesbylinat
From: Tiara

Lina, Can you hear my heart pounding out there in cyber space? I just tried to call you...you'll see my number on your caller ID, I know; yet I couldn't just scream into your answering machine which is what I really feel like doing!!!!! *&%$#@! Talk about feeling like a teenie-bopper! Remember how lately in my e-mails I've been saying how my days have been running between kid-crazed and ho-hum???? You'll never guess whom I got an e-mail from yesterday???? On the other hand, I know you've already guessed and you're 100% right!

Don't worry... I haven't replied yet and don't know whether I should. I can't believe he reached out even if it was a polite thank-you note. He did make reference to the fact that he was sorry my marriage was such a mess...he didn't use the word mess, I did. Anyway, I'd forward it to you but somehow that would feel 'sacrilegious'...even coming from heathen me! However, I will share with you his p.s. "You should stop feeling so self-conscious about your weight...a lot of men like their women 'Rubenesque.'

How's that for a no-calorie dreamsicle?!

Love,
me

Subj: Freeze!
Date: 3/18/02
From: linesbylina
To: Tiara

.   *Tia, Tia...mama-a-mia...time out...or time to freeze that dreamsicle and take a breath-NOT A LICK— though I know that's what you're dying to do about now if you haven't already! Anticipation, I know, though, will only make your craving stronger. Just take it slow, Tia...please.*

How is my god-daughter's tooth? Did Sam finish that science project Rory wrote me about? What about the band concert? Any or all of these questions ARE intended to take your mind off Margarita dreamsicles!!!!

Love,
me

Hot Dogs on the Mall...Not!

Subj: Risk
Date: 3/19/02
From: Tiara
To: Gabewing

Gabe, even though we exchanged e-mails, etc., I can honestly say I did not expect to hear from you and certainly not this soon. I enjoyed every minute of playing truant with you in Kemah and sharing what was going on in our lives. Bet you that getting back to work and your mind off those balmy Gulf golf links has been tough. After that relaxing warm week at Lina and Rod's, coming back (however glad to see my kids) was winter worst...hoping spring is almost here.

Tia

Tia took a deep breath and hit send. She wasn't going to run her reply past Lina or anyone. Damn it, she wasn't a kid and she didn't need anyone's permission. She felt a weight inside herself that she thought would lift once she replied. It was still there.

Or maybe it was that gynecologist appointment she made for next month.

Why had she promised Lina she would go??? She knew why... to get her off her back. She had made the huge slip in telling Lina she hadn't been in a couple of years. Yes, money was part of it...the kids always needed something and she felt great so why waste it???? Sadly and unbelievably enough, Tia had lost her closest cousin to that kind of cancer that was supposed to be so curable. It was years

35

ago and she had made a vow then that if she was ever attacked by any kind of cancer, she'd never let her family watch her slowly waste away. Especially not Meg, the daughter of her heart yet the natural child of her cousin who she and Rory had adopted as a toddler after Helena went to the other side. It was such a bittersweet time. Helena had been diagnosed with Hodgkins after she found out she was pregnant. She wouldn't tell a soul who the father was and she had refused any treatment until after Meg was safely born. By then it had been too late. They had slowly watched her waste away, lose her hair, watched her skin turn from its beautiful olive to gray to yellow, yet the glow of pride in her eyes when she held Meg was like a light that would never go out, especially when anyone who had known Helena, looked at Meg. The light was now there in her eyes shining with energy and life. Adopting Meg immediately was one of the few things she and Rory had ever agreed on. For years she had refused to allow herself to get pregnant by him, knowing deep inside she'd made a mistake. Then they had decided they didn't want Meg to be an only lonely, so they'd conceived Sam. She and Lina had these crazy code nick-names as middle schoolers. Lina's had been SAM (which stood for Smiling At Me) and Rory had agreed that was Sam, their gigantic smile of a child from the moment of his birth.. "Why?" she asked herself, 'was she thinking about all of this now?' Perhaps it was post trip blues or the lack of energy she'd been feeling off and on for months thinking it was just her body meeting menopause.

"Okay, Tia, pull yourself out of this black hole and get on with your day!"

There was an entire list of to-do's to tackle without sitting here losing time having a pity party.

3/20/02
Subj: Playing it Safe
From: Tiara
To: linesbylina

Lina,

FYI...finally replied to Gabe with a safe thank you e-mail...not more than five lines....so un-furrow your brow! Feeling a bit flat and really not sure why, yet I've got to move on with the day. Have a good one.

Love,
me

Subj: Magic
3/20/02 5:15 a.m.
To: linesbylina
From|: Ror7

Okay, how did you do it? Did you wave a magic wand or what? How did you get Tia to make a doctor's appointment for next month? I've been after her, yet have been told before in not so delicate terms to "butt out...that it's none of my business." The only reason I even know is because I saw it on the kitchen calendar. By the way, let her tell you herself...I think I've crossed a line by even telling you this much...however, did want to say thanks. I always said you were one of those white witches!

Subj: Wow
3/21/02 6:45 a.m.
To: Ror7
From: linesbylina

Rory, your secret is safe with me...I'm just glad she listened to me for once!!!! You want to know how I got that promise out of her...I plied her with wine during a 'sisterhood séance,' and my friend, those are more powerful than

Hallmark moments!

All kidding aside, she's just nuts to take risks like this at funky 50 when we have so many friends that have been bitten by the crab! Right now we just have to pray she actually goes through with the appointment, yet you can't say anything or you'll be the one who gets a bite taken out of you.

Love,
me

Subj: Ditto
3/22/02
From: Ror 7
To: linesbylina

Ditto, my friend!!! "Nuff said," as my kids say.
On a brighter pallete, your g-daughter really liked that link you sent her of that student artist's website. Forgive a prejudiced papa yet I think Meg really has talent and I hope she pursues her art....viewing your young friend's works on line and learning that she was using her gift to put herself through art school was really inspirational for both the dad and the daughter! Thanks for sending it to us!

Love,
me

The e-mails between the friends in cyber space encircled their lives like a merry-go-round with its ups, downs and in-betweens.

At Tia's it was the normal kids-stuff...Meg was finishing up after-school art lessons, developing into a young woman physically as well as emotionally.

It was a real challenge keeping Sam from teasing his sister about her bodacious 'tatas.' Maybe with the start of baseball season and all the practices it involved, he'd use up some of that burgeoning male testosterone energy. She and Rory pretty much lived their separate lives within the walls of their home, barely presenting a united front for the kids...backs turned from one another at night, they had not made love or even had sex in years.

Lina's house returned to it's relatively still state after spring break and Easter where she experienced her normal rush from doing a backlog of laundry (complete with armpit sweat stains-yuck), cooking all the boys' favorite meals, which had to include leftovers for take-back care packages, and dealing with the revolving door their schedules created whenever they were home. Lina thrived on the pace...she always maintained it kept her more organized and her time management at its peak. She was even looking forward to her first horseback lesson. Only one thing was niggling at the back of her mind, which was the fact that Tia had not mentioned the doctor's visit Rory said she'd put on their calendar. Now she wished she hadn't promised Rory she wouldn't say a word.

4/09/02
Subj: Cherry Blossoms
From: GabeWing
To: Tiara

Hi Tia,
        Hope you've readjusted since your trip. Just checking in to see how you're doing? How are Rory and the kids? Didn't want to totally lose touch after our reconnection and knew it was my turn at bat. If you ever cross the bridge, give me a call and we'll 'do lunch.'

Take care,
Gabe

Subj: Doing Lunch

4/10/02
From: Tiara
To: Gabewing

Gabe,

   As a matter of fact I have to 'cross the bridge,' as you put it, on Tuesday. If you really want to 'do lunch' how 'bout we nab a 'dog in the mall across from the National Art Gallery by the Carousel around 12:30. If you're busy, can't, or were just being polite, I totally understand.

Tia

Subj: Polite?
4/11/02
From: Gabewing
To: Tiara

Tia,

   Even though it has been years since we 're-met,' I think you know me way better than that! I don't do anything just to be polite. See you Tuesday at 12:30 by the Carousel...if something comes up, my cell is 404-232-0116.

Gabe

Shock?! There had to be a bigger, more powerful word for how she felt...or was she even feeling? Tia didn't even know how she had gotten herself from her doctor's office over to the gallery steps...yet this place had always given her a sense of comfort. Her mind or whatever automatic system her traitorous body put itself on got her here. Her thoughts were flying in every direction...the kids...her parents, sisters, Lina...she couldn't, wouldn't put them through this again.

Since Helena had died, she had a healthy respect for this horrific disease, this black bandit of life quality...somehow she had managed to think herself invincible. Hell, she had actually laughed at Lina's cautions about sunscreen and eating habits, saying that sometimes one had to eat to feed the soul, within reason. She may have binged on junk food once in a while, yet compared to most, she was decent about what she and her family put in their stomachs. When the doctor's office called last week to have her come back she should have realized...it just goes to show what an overwhelming distraction the combination of work and children can be. OR maybe she just hadn't wanted to face it...now there was no choice; talk about denial!!!!

Somehow she'd had the presence of mind to leave Gabe a message that she couldn't meet him and wanted to take a rain check on their impromptu lunch...

One of her favorite mantras or mottos which was taped, like other cards and pieces of inspiration, inside her kitchen cabinets was FAITH ISN'T FAITH UNTIL IT'S ALL YOU'RE HANGING ON TO...

The question was did she have faith in anything anymore? Right now she just needed some time...please, God...if you're there?

Subj: Raincheck
Date: 4/24/02
From: Tiara
To: Gabewing

Gabe,
  Sorry I had to bail on our lunch rendezvous last week. However, albeit the short notice, I'd like to take you up on the rain check for day after tomorrow same time, yet I would rather meet by the Phillips Gallery off Dupont Circle, if that's okay?

Thanks!

Tia
Subj: Same time, same place!
Date: 4/28/02
From: Gabewing
To: Tiara

See you Thursday—same time; the Phillips. Hope everything is okay.

Gabe

The Taste of Tears

05/01/2002

Rory,

When you read this, I'll be gone, though we both know we've not really been with each other in a very long time. However, this is not the time for word games or philosophy so please stay with me til the end of this letter...I can see you standing up pacing the room already.

You know I'm a woman of my word. If you'll recall the horrible time years ago when Helena was suffering through the end of her fight, I vowed I'd never let anyone I loved watch me suffer like that nor would I want to watch my own pain mirrored in their eyes. Yes, Rory, I have a form of cancer and it's at a questionable stage. And yes, I'm being selfish in many ways by removing myself from all of you and deciding to fight this, or not, on my own.

This is your big chance, Rory, with the kids. You always say that I've never allowed you freedom with them and treated you like a third child. Now is your time to take charge and move on with your own life while helping our children get through this. They are strong because the one thing we've both given them that we couldn't give to each other was pure unconditional love. I've written Meg and Sam a letter that I've left with this one.

They are going to be angry, so angry at first. Don't wallow in your own grief over this Rory with that tragic Irish side of yours. Put them first. I've left a list of three good counselors and already made you all a family appointment with the first one on the list for next week. No excuses Rory. Just go! Don't think about the money...think about all you'll be saving with me not having the credit card you've always accused me of over-using. (though I don't!!!) I have no right to ask you to promise anything, yet for the sake of the kids I am asking you to attend at least three sessions. None of you will want to go back after the first one. Please use the one step-at-a-time philosophy you're always espousing to me. Meg is going to need this especially...even though we adopted her when she was small and doesn't really remember Helena, she knows she lost her birth mother to cancer and now I've left her to face this...hopefully with you! Don't let her down. Don't let yourself down. If you fail Meg and Sam now, you will never forgive yourself later...and that will be more tragic than anything you've encountered.

I've taken $5000 dollars from each of the kids' college accounts. If I don't make it (and I'll see that something 'official' is sent to you), it will be more than paid back with the life insurance policy we've been paying on for years. If I do overcome this (and Rory, I do want to live), I promise you that it will be repaid in some way. Also, I've taken my name off the accounts and replaced it with yours.

Practically speaking, I've written out a list of the kids' schedules, sent letters to both of their school counselors explaining the situation, made you a prototype grocery list, laundry instructions, and generally anything I could think of to help you get started. There is also a 'To Whom I t May Concern' letter for you to use with a lawyer giving my consent to any type of divorce you wish to file.

Along with you and the kids, I sent a letter to my family and one to Lina. Rory, they will all rally round you. You can do this. While I've never been your cheerleader, like Lina, I do know deep within myself that you love Meg and Sam, who are the best part of any 'us.' Take care of them, Rory, and in taking care of them, you will be taking care of YOU.

You can do this, Rory.

Tia

Tia sighed and let out a deep breath…it felt as though she'd been holding her own since she started penning her words to Rory. Writing her parents and sisters had been tough, yet trying to make sense to Rory was the same challenge it always seemed to be, only now with a load of emotion and guilt weighing upon her like never before. Once again to herself she repeated the prayer she and Lina had learned in school so long ago, 'Guardian Angel, my guardian dear, to whom God's love commits me here. Ever this day be at my side, to light, to guard, to rule, to guide,' adding her own inner plea of 'Lord, please help me find the words for my children…'

Bittersweet

My Meg and Sam, ...

Yes, you'll always be my 'babies,' no matter how grownup you become or how old you are. This is probably the most difficult letter I've ever or will ever write because there is so much I want to share with you and despite what I say here, please know that deep inside myself I hope I will share it with you in person ...

First I want to ask your forgiveness for going away at this time. A few weeks ago a doctor told me that I have a form of cancer. Right now I am in the process of finding out if this is a kind that I can fight...and you know me, if I can fight something, I will. Have faith in that and the fact that there is nothing more I want to do than see the two of you grow up.

Though we don't talk about this very often because it's not an 'issue' as you young folk say, you both know we adopted Meg from my cousin Helena, whom you also know was one of my dearest friends along with Lina, when disease took her away from us. Watching her suffer at such a young age and worry about letting go of you, Meg, was unbelievably painful. As a mother, I naturally want to protect the two of you from witnessing any pain I might suffer or the changes my body will go through. If you're angry at first, I don't blame you one little bit. In many ways this is very selfish of me; yet the only reason I can walk away to deal with this, is because I know how very, very much Daddy loves you both. He will take care of you and love you and be there for you! In some ways, by leaving I'm sending out a message that says the people you love leave when the going gets tough. This is not true! You know I am a believer in that poem painted on the balloon in our bathroom that says children learn what they live.

Next week I've made an appointment with a family counselor I know through my work with Child Protective Services...she will help the two of you and Daddy deal with the sadness and the anger that will be all jumbled inside of you right now. When I wrote Daddy, I made him promise that you would all go at least three times together. Please help him keep that promise. Even if you're mad at me, do it for Dad!

Now you know I wouldn't go without a lecture lesson...and there are so many things I want to tell you about life...and I do hope I'll be lecturing these words in person sometime in the not too distant future...until then I hold you in my heart and ask you to read these words, listening as you do, because these things are like your painting pallet, Meg. All the different colors when put together in a certain way, create an image that reveals something...or like your computer designs Sam...you use different graphics and fonts and stuff I don't even begin to understand to make your cyber magic! So here goes...

The Golden Rule...no rolling your eyes, Sam!

It's true...treat other people the way you want to be treated...with love if you can.

Be aware...always. While the golden rule is the guideline on the right way to live, there are sick and twisted people out there who are not nice. I tell Aunt Lina she wears rose colored glasses meaning that she likes to focus on the good stuff. She's correct in choosing to look at the bright side of life, yet realize that over your shoulder or across the ocean or even down the street, bad things can be happening. Aunt Lina tells me in return that the glasses may be rose-tinted but they are not blinders!!!!!

Friends...this is a tough one. You are going to meet lots of people along life's path...some who are good; some who are 'cool,' some that are too good to be true, and some who turn you totally off. It's a piece of cake to be nice to the good ones and the cool ones; yet a real ball-buster (isn't that your word for challenge, Sam?) to be at least 'polite' (and you should always try to be) to the ones who turn you off. Here's a corny clue...a real friend will never ask you to do something illegal or something you know deep inside to be wrong. If they do, they are not reallllllllllly your friend.

Lina's mom used to say, "If your friends went and peed in the street, would you?" Poor Aunt Lina, she would cringe when her Mom talked with such bluntness...yet we never had any doubts about the message she was trying to relay. Another one of her rules or life lectures was don't put in writing what you wouldn't want the world to read. So you two...when you're writing those notes you pass to friends between classes, be careful what you say...and one day when you're writing love-letters be careful then too. Saying "I love you" can be so easy...it's showing it that's tough...like you guys giving me a quick kiss or hug g'bye when your friends are around 'cause giving ole mom a PDA (public display of affection) just isn't done, right???!!

Speaking of love, don't confuse it with sex!!! Meg I can see you blushing and Sam are your hands covering your face?! Gotcha! Come on guys...you need to get real here. One day you're both going to want to 'get physical' as they used to say in my day with a member of the opposite sex. If you're drawn to that person, it's going to feeeeeeel gooooooood...it's supposed to! Don't be ashamed of that fact; yet don't confuse it with love. In your great grandmother's day they had a saying "Why buy the cow when you can get the milk for free?" The Woodstock generation took it to another level and I hope your generation—learns to differentiate the feelings from the 'feeling' if you get my drift. If you don't, well...Dad or Aunt Lina will just have to elaborate...and if you think I tell it like it is....remember it was Aunt Lina who had everyone in her

Sunday school class pass around condoms and tampons when she was teaching sex education! Don't worry though...I think just she does it for the shock affect!

My writer's cramp is telling me this is getting waaaaaaay toooo long and you're probably frustrated at my attempts to be witty so Ill wrap it up for now with education...in this area I hope you'll go all the way. College just isn't about grades and learning the academics, though those are fundamentally (look it up!) important. College life is another stage of growing up, a proving ground for adulthood... a place to tie it all together. Don't waste your Dad's hard earned money by thinking it's a time to part-tee! You each need to grow up and find out who you are before you decide to share life with someone else. Even though Dad and I disagree on a lot of things,(as you know we do!), we both wish we had done a lot more growing into our own skins before we got married.

We both love you two more than anyone or anything...

I LOVE YOU WITH ALL MY HEART AND SOUL...more than you'll ever know...and I'm going to be trying...don't for a minute think I'm giving up on you or on life!!! The key is balance in all things...eating, 'drinking,' learning, loving. (I believe in all those quirky little sayings I've gotten taped inside of all our kitchen cabinets...I really do!)

Every minute of every day, you'll be with me in my heart and I'll be with you in yours...(Remember 'Littlefoot' the Dinosaur) don't doubt for a minute that I'm there. I am.

All my love,
Mom

Neverland

Subj: En route to Neverland
From: Tiara
To: linesbylina

Lina,

If I worked the 'send later' mode correctly, you'll be receiving this as I'm on my flight to 'Neverland.' Sorry. Really, I don't mean to sound so cryptic and I would have preferred 'snail mail,' as my aunt calls it or a real letter to an e-mail, yet by the time Rory, the kids, and my family read the letters I've written them, you will have been called and heard their justifiably hysterical words. My white-lie to them was that I told them I sent you a letter too...and it is a letter, rather it's just an e-mail letter.

Remember when we were in the hot tub and I talked about a 'free pass?' Well, you know the saying, "Be careful what you pray for?" It has come to pass—pun intended! Writing to you at this moment is somewhat like I'd imagine an out-of-body experience...so forgive my attempts at levity. Helena was my cousin and if I'm honest, your dearest friend (something I was once jealous of for a long time)...watching her suffer as disease ate away at her body and sometimes her spirit was one of the most pain-filled experiences of my life and I vowed if that dreaded disease ever got me, I'd not let anyone I loved watch me disappear in slow motion the same way. I'll never forget watching her gasp for breath that last day and still trying to smile for Meg.

Lina, I know you won't take a bit of satisfaction or even

think an 'I told you so,' yet my friend you were so right when you told me during our visit this winter that I was not immune to life's curses, no matter how I liked to fly in the face of the wind. About a month after getting back, I did go for the *%$#?! doctor's visit I promised you. Walked out of that office, relieved it was over with and never gave it a second thought until I got THE CALL. Brace yourself Lina and don't fall apart on me!

My body is a traitor and I've been diagnosed with an advanced stage of a rare type of blood related cancer (at least I'm unique). Treatments for this are in an experimental stage and being a risk taker, I volunteered to be a guinea pig. Don't cry, Lina...I'm okay, really—or as okay as I can be right now and this moment is all that counts. At first I wasn't...I was in such shock and so damn angry with God, with everything, and with YOU for making me promise to go to the doctor. When a doctor tells you that "you have cancer," those are not the words you hear. What you hear is "Oh my God, I'm going to die." I'm trying to get past most of that....

Breathe, I tell myself...now to practical matters... Rory will be calling you or e-mailing you...though I think he'll call. Selfishly, I've run away from home. I just can't be with him during this or I know I'll take out every ounce of my anger on him. Recall, my friend, when your Mom was dying last Fall...think about how upset you would get because she'd rant and scream at your Dad, your brother and your sweet sister-in-law who were just trying to take care of her and make her last months less painful. We knew she was just venting yet it didn't make it any the less abrasive. Your parents had a 50-year marriage!!!! Rory and I have had nothing between us for a long while now. My hope is to be in touch again because I need you! However, I need you sane and together and supporting me in this...not trying to talk me into going back to 'people who love me.' Lina, I'm warning you now if you send me a return e-mail with any of that type rhetoric or any of your column advice, you won't hear from me again unless I get better. This warning is coming at you this one time, my friend, because I literally don't have the emotional energy and have been told that soon I won't have it physically either.

Lina, I am going to fight this; not your way-my way. After some pretty grueling tests, unbelievably I was accepted into an experimental program.

Don't ask me why, Lina, yet some spirit is watching over me because when I made the initial doctor's appointment I set it up with a new female physician I'd heard about through one of the women in my yoga class. When I went for the actual checkup I used a false last name and paid cash. It's weird, Lina, yet I even lied on the forms saying I was single and in the past medical history I checked miscarriage. You chuckle at my mystic vibes yet these white lies may be my lifeline. If they knew I was married or had kids I would have never been eligible to be part of this experimental program.

Because of our history, Lina, I know how your practical mind-set is working overtime to figure out how I will ever get away with this. Gabe has become my knight...not in the sense I fantasized about; yet as a friend who was there when I needed one. It's obviously a long story, the details of which I cannot go into now. The day I found out, I was supposed to have met Gabe for a hotdog lunch on the Mall. Needless to say I was in no mood for food of any kind, even a dreamsicle so I left a message at his office saying something came up and could I take a rain-check.

After I found out that I could be accepted into the program which is not here, I panicked, knowing I had no ID to back me up so I called Gabe, asking if I could collect on the raincheck. I met him in front of the Phillips (Lina, I know that's 'our' place, yet it gives me such an immortal feeling so forgive me for sharing it with him). It's funny how in a place like that which is open to strangers, almost like a church, you can be anonymous within the mass. As always, I got there *early to visit 'The Boating Party' for you. You know Gabe is with the Bureau, yet he used to be with police, and has some good connections with law enforcement folk and sources, who are...let's say a tad bit outside the law. Literally I threw myself on his mercy and asked him if he could get one of his buddies to get me a fake ID, etc. At first, his self-righteous FBI Agent side was having no part of my lil' scheme-even if it was truly life or death. My temper got the best of me and I literally told him to &^%$# off and that I'd get my own help through some of the drug guys I deal with through my counseling work. Lina, the tears were streaming down my face as I stomped toward the Dupont Circle subway...feeling let down by everything and everyone. Then I heard running and turned around...to make a long story short, he has helped me in numerous ways.*

Don't call him Lina...he's NOT going to tell you where I am or who I am.

Even though he didn't actually pull the strings to do this for me, he could still get fired or worse for 'aiding and abetting,' so just don't! And sister-swear, not a single word to Rory about Gabe's assistance in this...his ego and self esteem will be low enough. Telling him I allowed another male to come to the rescue will not help him or this precarious situation one bit.

Lina, I'm going to attach the letters I left Rory and the kids (though I handwrote the one I left to Meg and Sam)... you are my sister-friend...and the only reason I'm sharing my words to them with you is that I think, no I know—they are really going to need you!!!! Without a doubt, I know too that you'll be there for them. Lina, this IS Rory's 'free pass.' For God's sake, please encourage him to take it and pleassssssssssssssse, Lina, make him take the kids to the counselor—they will all need help with my escape to 'Neverland,' whether it's a visit or forever. Selfishly, I wanted to spare them the pain and the ugliness of this. No doubt there will be fallout in terms of the anger and betrayal they will naturally feel...hopefully in time the right help will get them past it.

Hang in there...take deep breaths, too...let Rod and Gracie help you; let your mentor friend there in Texas. Just let them all think you got a 'au revoir' letter like everyone else. If I find you've betrayed me in this, no matter how well intentioned you think your motives are, you won't hear from me again.

I love you,
me

Lina stared out at the lake, Tia's e-mail printed out on her lap...she had read it and reread it at least twenty times, if not more. She really could not believe this, yet knowing Tia as she did, it was true. She knew too that Tia did not make idle threats. Lina swore she could almost feel Tia's fear, her pain and yes, the despair. Conversely, her gut told her Tia was a fighter and a survivor. If anyone could overcome death-defying odds, it was Tia. Lina only wished she had trusted her enough to clue her in before she left for wherever it was she was going. Now all she could do was wait for Rory to call. Lina would not risk getting in touch with Gabe, YET.

Twenty-four hours had not passed since she read Tia's words when the phone rang. Picking it up, she saw by the caller ID that it was indeed Rory.

Taking a deep breath, she answered, "Hello."

"Okay, Lina, where is she?"

"Rory! (God forgive me these white lies I'm about to tell!) You must be pulling your hair out. This morning a Fed-Ex package arrived with a letter from Tia. I've been in shock all day. She told me what she had done. How are the kids?"

"Lina, cut the crap. I know she told you what she's up to...she tells you everything."

"Rory, honestly, this time I'm as in the dark as you (almost!). Are you okay? Meg and Sam?"

"Lina, I just read her 'Dear John' and after 27 plus years of marriage, even if the last ten have sucked, I think I deserve a more personal exit, not to mention the fact that I'm worried sick about her. I cannot believe she did this. I called her regular doctor and they swear they have not seen her. And our kids!!! Tia has always been such a tigress about the kids, how in the hell could she do this to them??!!! All those words about not wanting them to watch her suffer…that's bullshit and you know it. How am I??! I'm mad, yes, mad, not just angry… and I can't believe she has the balls to ask me to make promises about the kids, counselors. On top of that she has the guts to leave me lists, schedules…" With that Rory's voice broke into angry sobs.

Tia, how could you leave me with this mess, Lina thought and then chastised herself for the selfishness of what she was thinking.

"Rory, hang in there. I'll fly out for the weekend. In the letter she sent me she told me she had made you a counselor's appointment for next Monday. I'll stay til after that. While I'll be the first to admit what she's done is crazy and selfish and totally off the wall, it is *so* Tia! We have to think of Meg and Sam. And, Rory, we also have to think of Tia's state of mind. She's afraid and she's a fighter, so right now she's just swinging her arms at life and trying to tread water in a stormy sea. Please calm down now and tell me how the kids are taking this."

"Lina, how in the hell do you think they are taking this?! Your god-daughter's red rimmed eyes have fire in them yet she's being a trooper sitting in the TV room with her arms around Sam who I don't think has digested this fully. When she came into the kitchen to get Sam some water she told me she wasn't going to give Mom the satisfaction of going to any counselor. Lina, she's 15 years old and she's pissed. Like her, I don't think visiting a counselor is going to be the magic wand that removes the sense of being deserted we all feel. I'm taking the next couple of days off to regroup. Hell, Lina, she took every single personal item of hers from our bedroom with her or else she has it stored somewhere."

"Rory, I am so sorry…I just have no words. Call me day or night to listen. I'll e-mail you tomorrow with my flight number…I'll leave Friday night and try to get a flight back out late Monday. Between us, we do need to make sure that appointment is met. It's the right thing to do, Rory, and you know it."

"Lina, I'll think about it, yet I'm not making any promises. I know the kids will be glad to see you and need your hugs right now so please know I appreciate the fact that you'll be here. Tell Rod I said thanks for letting us borrow you…I'll check you on the net tomorrow for the flight info."

"Bye Rory…I love you all."

Memories Pressed Against the Pages of My Mind

Lina placed the phone on the receiver and the tears she had been holding back just poured forth, the sobs shaking her body until she felt bone dry…it felt like she was crying for Helena, her Mom and everyone who she had ever loved and lost to this silent, cell eating monster. She remembered when she wrote Microsoft after her friend Karina died and her young son was dealing with such anger. She wanted them to invent a pac-man type game where the kids could electronically devour cancer cells instead. Microsoft had replied thanks, but no thanks…they didn't think there was a market. Hah…she knew way too many victims of this disease with youngsters who needed an outlet for their pain…now it was going to hurt Meg and Sam.

"Why, God, why" she relentlessly turned to Him with her anger demanding to know why we are put on this earth only to be yanked away.

Last year, when she had received a recognition award for her work in the community and had to walk up to the podium… something she was never any good at… she remembered she had addressed the blur of faces with these words. "When the nuns teaching us in school threw out this catechism question: Why did God make me? The answer was this: 'God made me to know, love and serve Him in this world to be happy with Him in the next.' It has been my honor to serve you." She remembered taking her seat to the applause and wondering how those words had ever come to her at that moment. Why was she recalling them now?

Lina got up, splashed her face with cold water, and then went to her office to look up a journal entry. Her journals were never consistent…and they weren't really journals per say, more a conglomeration of her own written reflections and poems, as well as e-mail print-outs between she and friends that she kept in notebooks from year to year. For some reason it entered her mind that back in January she had been in a post holiday funk, traveling memory lane and writing about her and Tia. Something was drawing her back to those particular words…

Journaling in January 2002

It was a quarter past Christmas, the decorations were down; the boys, blessedly good students, were back at school. The girls, successful in their workaday world, were settled in places and lives of their own; and the quiet she had always thought she craved was louder than any boom box. The passing of time hadn't really pestered her. And even though the ole' biological clock is pointing toward the funky fifties, in some ways I feel like the little girl who delighted in the wind tickling her hair with the warm planks of a Chesapeake pier under the tender feet of her childhood.

The home front was organized, the house itself tasteful, tidy, and bright. My column and community work on task. Yet ever since Fall, the kite of my life, which usually whipped this way and that, wanting to soar in joy and hope, was finding no breeze strong enough to give it lift...no wave forceful enough to break the tide of human emotions spiraling out of control.

Fate took my dearest friend too early and gifted me with a baby boy-my own personal rainbow along with the other three jewels whom I'm honored to 'mother.' This past November, my mother who had always challenged me by never quite approving left a void I can't quite understand. Growing older, making or not making 'your' mark on the world? Could it be that simple or that complicated?

Closing her eyes
It was a kaleidoscope of memories
A Grandmother's second floor dress shop
Papa's ground level gifts
Skipping to the 'Boys' Deli
A nickel in her palm

For a candy bar or crusty bread, it didn't matter
Flick o' the wrist-the colors and scene change
Pippin Lane, the haphazard hobby farm next door
Babysitting for the young neighbors
Finding validation in bringing order to their chaos

Walks to and from St. Boscos'
Those nuns in black with milk cartons atop their heads
Three knots hanging down from their robes
Franciscan ladies who could be gentle and loving
Or even twisted in their discipline, ruling for the Lord!

Turn the scope again...
Summers at the Bay, a sandy beach, the rock wall,
Riding the bow with its baptism of sticky salty spray
Long all night rides in the back of the station wagon
Family reunions South with grown up cousins who knew
about makeup
St. Theresa's High School...bus rides to and from the city
All pieces of the puzzle
Threads of living's tangled tapestry that somehow transforms
itself
Into core moments that let you know this is why you were born
Ah, life!

So what now? Was there time to make a mark? Has it passed me
by? Was there going to be a dramatic fateful moment to break the
tide, to give lift to the kite?????
Even though Tia had always been challenging, I didn't expect the
shocked reaction to a comment I had made during a recent phone
visit that, "I haven't really listened to music since that time...you
know, what I'm talking about, Tia. I just don't." One of Tia's lifelines
in her complicated life was song. In fact for a while I had this card
framed that Tina sent long ago of a baby grand piano, balloons
floating out of it, with words printed on it to the affect 'music sets free

the corners of the soul.'

Typically, like a country western song, a lot of music was either a story of love failed, which was painful, or of a love found. Tia thinks I've felt regret for having believed in a dream, yet that wasn't really the truth. No, I could never regret the free flying, rollin-down-a-hill feeling that typified that time in my life all those years ago...or at least that's how it felt for a while. That roller coaster time was like a prized treasure, now tucked away, because like all diamonds, it had its price.

This comfort zone I have now is one I've earned and Tia's understanding of that fact means more than she'll ever know. Tia doesn't try to convert me to her way of facing life and her defiant dramatic way of facing the storm. I don't want to tie myself to the mast and let the wind and water tear at me so I can grieve for all the dreams let go. New dreams and new songs are what I want. How to find them? Those bittersweet years taught me. Fate doesn't just hand them over like a gift.

Tia would buy something to please herself in a heartbeat and I would too—within reason; though Tia didn't quite see it that way. Where did she think all the little things, the carefully placed objects de art or fun knick-knacks around the house had come from? Then again, Tia would never deny herself the way I've had to in the past, or discipline herself to the routine 8 to 5 world that slowly yet surely created an intangible that I cannot quite explain...the view of the pond out the back window, the ducks' rippling wake was its own ballet. While I'm led by the voice within that only listening to the silence whispers, Tia moves to the beat. Perhaps I need to admit that I don't really listen to the chorus of angels reminding me that I can 'dance' again.

Lina put the journal down...she had goose bumps and it wasn't from a chill in the air. She couldn't wait til Rod came home...she needed the comfort of his arms as she wondered where Tia was, what she was feeling and if she was okay. Please God let her be okay.

Safe Landings

Subj: Safe and Sound
5/4/02
From: Tiara@netsong.com
To: Gabewing

Gabe,

Just a quick note to let you know I arrived safely, found the lodgings you so kindly found me, had my initial tests and blood work. It looks like things are a go for the end of next week. Right now my focus is on getting a cell phone, finding a low-key part-time job (they said I should be able to work a few hours a day for a while), set up a checking account and generally get on with the mechanics of life…I miss my kids and am so terribly worried about them…at times I've wondered if I'll be able to go through with this…I need Lina to be my eyes and ears and am just praying the weight of this deception won't be too much for her or our friendship to carry. Saying thank you just seems like the understatement of the year.

With love and eternal gratitude,
Tia

Subj: Arrived
5/4/02
From: Tiara@netsong.com
To: linesbylina

Lina.

Note my new e-mail, which I'll access from one of those internet cafes once or twice a week. Hope you're okay…I've arrived at my destination, have lodgings and have had initial tests and blood work done. If all goes well, treatment commences next week.How are my kids??????? By now Rory has called you. Please let me be able to trust you…I know asking you to be the link to my family is placing a heavy burden on our friendship though if our places were reversed, I would do this for you…in a heartbeat.

Love,
Me

Subj: In a Heartbeat!
5/4/02
From: linesbylina
To: Tiara @netsong.com

Tia,

Thank heavens you're settled somewhere…I've, no— we've all been worried sick. You're right…this deception, albeit done for good reasons, is one huge boulder!!!! You made me promise no lectures…so I hope you appreciate the fact that my tongue looks like a sieve from biting it!

Last weekend I flew out to be with Rory and the kids…they are ANGRY, Tia…very, very angry and worried about you, naturally. Rory's ego is sorely bruised yet the emptiness that has existed between the two of you for so long will end up being his life-preserver. Sam, though he is very upset, will get past this eventually, as Rory and Meg are all over him with love, affection and defense of you. Meg is another story, my friend, and I hate to add to your load yet your daughter, my godchild, is going to have a much tougher time getting through this than anyone.

Meg is in the no-zone between childhood and adulthood. Because of Helena, she's not counting on a happily ever after; and her fear of losing you for good is of monstrous proportions.

They did go to the counselor last Monday, though Meg originally had said she was not going to give you the 'satisfaction.' Scheduled my flight out late on Monday primarily because I was afraid they'd all no-show if I wasn't there to push them through the door. Meg went to the session totally for her Dad and Sam...that child has a big heart, around which she's working hard to construct steel magnolia walls. Who can blame her? The counselor must have seen her squeezing my hand or picked up on something and suggested that Meg e-mail me at least once a week to vent her feelings and barring that, she suggested a journal. For Sam she recommended a punching bag (an object on which he could take out his anger) and addressing Rory she asked that he think about a second appointment for them all. She was good, Tia, very good and I do hope for their own health and welfare, as much as yours, they'll go back. Meg didn't commit to anything there. When we left the appointment I suggested ice cream cones (soul food as you might say) and then commandeered them straight to a sporting goods store where I 'treated' to the punching bag. Rory promised me he'd hang it up in the garage. I'm going to leave them be for a week or so before calling or e-mailing ...they need to simmer and settle.

Can you at least tell me where you are? Is there anything you need?

Love,
me

Tia lay across the bed, a tepid washrag across her forehead. The generator for the air conditioner created an almost mantra-like hum that might have been relaxing if it weren't for the sway and pitching of her stomach or was it the boat? Three months ago when Gabe arranged this residence for her, just an hour from the hospital, living on a luxury sailboat, free of rent, sounded like a great idea. Right now she wasn't so sure...then again she wasn't sure of anything. Her hair had begun to fall out. Think positive, she admonished herself...no gray; and she'd lost six pounds. Ironically, she remembered telling Lina and Gabe she wanted to lose 15 pounds.

She needed to get herself up and walk over from the marina with her parasol to the shop where she had lucked into a nearly perfect part-time job. The owner, Ann, was a doll, working with her on a flexible schedule and letting her use her computer to e-mail Lina so she could keep tabs on her kids. It was just enough to keep her in groceries (not that she was eating much), and pay for the few expenses she had without having to use any more of the money she took from the kids' education accounts. The fresh air, albeit HOT, would do her good and she wanted to keep to her work schedule for as long as she could. Ann had already been too kind about juggling shifts as it was. Tia knew, though, that her angel of a boss understood, being a breast cancer survivor herself.

Something had drawn her to the little shop the day after she settled into her temporary floating home, or maybe it was just the pink flamingo flag flying in front of it that brought back thoughts of Lina's flamingo by the hot tub! Once through that door, she and Ann had immediately connected. Over and above the employer-employee relationship, they had spent quite a few evenings at the picnic table out back after work, talking and sharing the details of living while facing one's fears day by day

Sleeping Beauty

Gabe couldn't wait any longer. The last e-mail he had received said she might not be in touch for a while because the 'white coats' anticipated her having more of a reaction after the next round of treatment. It had already been a bit over two weeks. Tia was just so darned independent and didn't want to ask anyone for help. He practically had to use brute force to get her to accept his gift of the car he rented for her so that she could travel to and from the hospital without a hassle...now he was worried about her ability to even drive. Lord, he hoped he had done the right thing in supporting her in this healing sabbatical as she termed it. Communicating with the big guy upstairs was something he hadn't done a lot of in years, yet this past Lent he found himself going to church again and praying for Tia, that this treatment would work and that she'd be her healthy, whole spunky self again.

Tia had attracted him from the first time he saw her in front the apartments skipping rope with some little neighborhood girls who were doing some kind of intricate sing-song jump-roping! Man! She had been one determined lil' lady and he remembered standing there just laughing. They'd introduced themselves and that's when he learned that she and her husband lived in the complex. He remembered thinking 'All the good ones are married!' Gabe respected the institution, despite today's statistics, and therefore always kept an arm's length. He liked Rory yet had thought from the get-go that he and Tia were like gears that just didn't work in sync. When she came up with this plan, she told him she had left Rory a letter saying she wouldn't stand in his way of a divorce. However, that wasn't a done deal, and for now, all he wanted to do was support her through this time so she could get well and get back to those kids she so desperately missed.

The salt air always gave him an immediate feel of relaxation and as his tires crunched over the pebbles of the marina driveway, he hoped living on the water had been therapeutic for Tia as well. He also didn't want to startle her by surprising her this way. Yet what better excuse than the long July4th weekend and wanting to see fireworks reflected in the water! In his own defense, he had tried several times to reach her by cell to give her a heads up about this visit. Actually, he didn't think she ever turned the thing on!!!

Removing a duffle from the trunk of the rental jeep, he walked toward Pier K. 'Mysts' was a beauty, a 42-foot Moody. His friend, Jack, who owned her, had more dinero than common sense, only sailing her a couple of weeks a year or using her as a occasional business party backdrop. Nevertheless, he had always appreciated Jack's generosity in lending her out, no questions asked. Though Gabe didn't have a lot of what he termed friends, the ones he did have were the real deal.

It was so quiet…he didn't even hear a radio. In the past Tia always had music of some type or other playing in the background.

"Yo…Is the Captain aboard this vessel?" The only reply he got was the squawk of a gull flying over.

He opened the canvas hatch…she should really lock this baby up when she leaves, he thought. Lowering himself down the cabin ladder, he was overcome with the feeling that she was on board.

"Tia, you down here? It's Gabe!"

No answer.

There was an open container of crackers on the minuscule counter and a few dishes in the sink; a sweatshirt thrown across table. The door to the master cabin was partially closed. Maybe she was asleep. He tapped the door lightly…then slowly pushed it open.

Swallowing and feeling emotion overtake him, he was glad she was sleeping so soundly. He knew he could not have hidden the shock that had to have crossed his face upon seeing her for the first time since she left in early May. She was so pale. Tia with that glowing olive skin was now translucent. Her head was shaved; yet strangely that wasn't as bad as he had imagined. Her face looked so different. What was it? He knew he shouldn't stand there and stare yet at the same time he felt absolutely rooted to the spot studying her like she was a work of art. It was her eyes. Her shapely brows and lovely lashes were gone. She appeared so small and defenseless. The Tia he knew would never be defenseless. She had lost weight. Well, that must make her happy, he thought. He remembered when they ran into each other this past winter and how adamant she was about her intent to lose her forties-fifties flesh, as she termed it. He remembered telling her he liked Rubenesque women.

Okay, Gabe, get a grip on your mind, man and back up. Leave the woman some pride. Silently, he went to the cabin at the opposite end of the boat and threw his duffle in the storage beneath the bunk. Turning back around toward the ladder he saw a couple of photos pinned to a small bulletin board. Taking a closer look, he knew these must be of Meg and Sam. Smiling, he thought Sam looked every bit the happy-go-lucky adolescent Tia had described; and Meg, well she was going to be a beauty one day. Being away from them had to be tearing her apart. In his book, she was such a trooper; insisting on sending him a check for Jack each month to cover the utilities, and working that part-time job. Right now she looked like a good breeze could knock her over.

Trying to shake his thoughts loose, he decided to check out the 'frig. A grocery run was definitely in line. Then he'd come back and start this visit over.

Docksiders

Tia looked at the clock...11:50 a.m.?! The anti-nausea meds really put her out. Still, it felt good to sleep so soundly for once. Slowly, she edged herself off the bed, trying to get her equilibrium before she tried the shower. The warm water was going to feel good though she usually had to sit back down after her time under the spray. She couldn't believe what she used to take for granted...like energy, like doing two tasks in a row without resting in between, like a good healthy appetite with cravings! This 'yuck' gave the adage 'the grass is always greener on the other side' new meaning...a double meaning in fact, because about eighty-percent of the time she felt and even swore she looked green!

Dressed, bandana'd (paisley today) and sipping a cup of tea, she felt the boat move and heard steps on the stern.

"Ahoy!!! Man Aboard! Is there a damsel in distress on this vessel?"

"Gabe?" she called out, recognizing his voice. No sooner said than a pair of muscular tanned legs appeared on the ladder.

He grinned, a grocery sack in one arm and a bouquet of sunflowers and daisies in the other.

"What balance," she quipped before covering her face with her hands and sinking further into the cushioned bench. "I look terrible and didn't want you to see me like this. You're just lucky I'm up, dressed and have my q-ball of a head covered or you would have thought you just descended the mummy's tomb."

Gabe put the flowers on the table in front of her and sat the sack down. Gently, he lifted her from the elbows and wrapped her in a comforting hug.

"Woman, you're not down here for sun and spa time. You're sick and allowed to have an original look right now."

The warmth of human contact felt so good. Savoring the feeling and talking into his broad chest, Tia chuckled, "Original? Aren't you getting to be politically correct or is it a diplomatic career you're focused on?! Seriously, Gabe, what are you doing here?????"

Regretfully letting go and backing away a bit for fear she would hear his heartbeat, Gabe quipped back, "Hey, can't a guy visit a friend and take a few days off over a long weekend to sip Margaritas on the back of a sailboat? I've got tons of leave and if I don't use it, I lose it."

"Yeah, right!"

Reaching out with a brief touch to her face he said, "Okay, Tia, I was worried about you since I hadn't heard from you in a couple of weeks and tried calling your cell more than a couple of times. Do you ever turn the thing on?"

"Actually, no I don't...not unless I'm going to use it, which is rare. Picking up the bouquet and looking up at him with smiling eyes, she said, "These are just beautiful; thank you. Did you know sunflowers mean obedience? They are Lina's absolute favorite and I really like them too. Now if I can just find a container to put them in. So, what's in the grocery bag?"

"Just this and that-my feeble yet honorable attempt to tickle your taste buds."

" If you can tickle my taste buds, then I'd say you're a magician disguised as an FBI Agent. Let's see what you've got Houdini."

Sweeping an arm towards the sack with a bow, "Voila, Madame...Popsicles!! One of my buddies at the agency whose wife had been undergoing treatment for breast cancer last year told me that when nothing else would stay down, these would. So tonight while I'm sipping a Margarita on the stern you can relax with one of these. Not knowing your flavor preference, I got a variety pack!"

"So far, so good. I'm impressed. What else"

"Not much really...some chicken noodle soup, melba toast, bananas... just a buffet of easy on the system stuff for you to try when I'm not around to wine and dine you. Tia, if you're up to it, tonight

I'd like to take you out."

"Gabe, I appreciate all this really, I just don't know if I'm up to fine dining in public, especially with the holiday crowds."

"The crowds won't be in force 'til tomorrow, and it doesn't have to be anything fancy...just somewhere we can watch the boats come in at sunset and talk. Sound good?"

"To be honest, nothing really sounds good; though having some out-loud table talk is more than just a little bit appealing, I must admit... So how long do I get the pleasure of your company and are you staying here on the boat with me?"

"Just through the weekend, and yes, if it's okay, I was going to bunk in the other cabin. Getting a hotel room is no problem, though. I made a reservation just in case. All I need to do is cancel or confirm it."

"Gabe, don't be silly! Cancel the reservation! After all you've done for me!!! You'll have to excuse me for a nap this afternoon, though, if we're going out later, though. Obviously, I need all the beauty sleep I can get."

"Tia, you're way too hard on yourself...if you don't wake up on your own, I'll wake you up around five-ish, sleeping beauty. Now git." With a flip of the wrist, he motioned toward her cabin.

With no energy to argue, Tia did as she was directed, making her way steadily towards the cabin just three giant steps away. For Gabe's sake, Tia tried to put some bounce in her step.

Then turning towards Gabe, she gave him one last smile before stepping through the opening and closing the door that stood between them. Her heart actually felt lighter than it had in months...

Magic Mirror On the Wall

It felt so good to be out in public, among people, eating real food, watching summer sailors with their boats and yachts coming in off the bay, toasted, one way or another, she thought to herself and chuckled.

"What's got you smiling to yourself...you look like the cat that ate the canary."

"Oh, I was just smirking over the wide array of toast out there."

" Toast?"

"Yeah...these mariners coming in off the water look either sun toasted or 'toast' toasted as in self-marinated. It's hard to believe that just this morning I was rolling in self pity. Now I'm sitting on the deck of the restaurant where I first saw you after all those years. What's harder to believe is all that's happened since February. Without your support, how could I have ever survived what's going on in my life?"

"Tia, you would have been fine because you ARE a survivor. Hey, I'm just glad that you're fighting this monster and that you were able to get this treatment. Lifting his Margarita, "Here's to surviving and living well!"

"Amen to that!" smiled Tia.

"By the way, lady, did I tell you how chic you looked in your bandana, straw hat and sunglasses...kind of Garbo gone to the Beach!"

"Right this moment I actually feel great. There's something to that saying 'mood follows action.' Sometimes the last thing you feel like with this gunk in your system is putting gunk on your face yet it felt good to look in the mirror and see my reflection appear almost human again. Two years ago, I think, Lina actually wrote an article about cancer patients and looking better to feel better. At the time I didn't buy into it and thought it was more of her Pollyanna idealism. This evening is an example of it making sense. It's simply a matter of getting yourself to do it."

"Okay, so next week when you're alone, remember tonight and maybe it will give you the incentive to repeat the feeling."

It's more than just the makeup and the food making me feel good, she thought to herself.

Nibbling a chip and toying with the tortillia soup left in her bowl she asked, "How's the lobster?"

"It's delicious. I just feel bad you don't have the appetite for something more exciting."

"Whadya mean? This is the most excitement I've had in weeks and the soup actually feels like it's going to stay down, which is exciting in itself…must be the good company seasoning."

"Enough with the surface banter…My gender, I know is not known for diving into the emotional deep, yet, Tia, I really want to know how you are. While beating around the bush isn't my usual modus operandi, I guess I've been too hesitant to come right out and ask …so… are you afraid? What do you think about in the middle of the night when you're awake all alone?"

"Of course I'm scared! I wake up and ask myself if I will see my kids at Christmas? Will I even be alive? Is there a God? How are the kids doing in school? If I do make it, how will I tell Rory I just can't go back to us. Mostly, Gabe, I just don't let myself think…I've been keeping a journal and playing with thoughts for the book I've always wanted to write. I miss having a computer at my disposal. Much of the time, I don't even feel like doing anything at all. My energy level is low to say the least and my mind seems to take trips away from me. Sometimes I can't remember what I've said out loud and what I've thought. Like now…flipping subjects like Sam channel surfs. When I do feel fairly good, I try to relieve Ann at the shop. She's been so wonderful letting me make my hours there. In fact, the two of you and Lina are my lifelines.

In response he just gave her hand a gentle squeeze. "Tia, I can't do much about the middle of the night monsters of doubt and loneliness, unless of course you should decide to use that cell phone and call…I've told you I'm available any time. However, I did bring you a little surprise."

"Gabe, you've already done enough…I don't need any more surprises!"

"Listen, it's not that big a deal…just my old laptop. It's probably not good for anything other than word-processing and e-mail. I was going to get you online before I left…at least now you won't have to wait til you're at the shop to send messages."

Speechless for a moment, Tia actually felt like her cup runneth over, and she hadn't experienced that particular feeling in a long while, especially since she found out about her illness, "Gabe, I don't know what to say…thank you so much!"

"You don't need to say anything…C'mon, let's call it an evening and get you tucked in."

Just as they were standing to leave, Tia practically fell back down into her chair. "Did you hear that?"

"What????"

"Oh, My God! I can't believe this…Gabe don't look over toward the Flying Dutchman… put your sunglasses on and your baseball cap."

"Tia, what in the hell?"

"Just do it Gabe, please."

Gabe pulled the sunglasses he had hanging in the neck of his shirt out and slowly put them on. Then he reached into his back pocket to pull out the scruffy hat she had teased him about wearing in the first place. The entire time he was looking at Tia who was biting her lip. This suspense felt like slow motion yet it was a matter of seconds…

Now look over…you're not going to believe it…it's Rory and the kids with Lina and Rod."

Sam was pointing up at a seagull that had nabbed some food off his plate, obviously thinking it was a hoot. Meg and the others were just laughing with him. Tears started to silently streak Tia's face. "They look so happy and carefree," she whispered.

"They look like great kids, Tia. You sure you just don't want to walk over there and give up this charade?"

"Not at all, Gabe; if anything, it makes me more determined than ever to protect them from seeing me with this ravaged body."

"They're tougher and more resilient than you think."

"Oh yeah, and you know this from experience with your own the kids," she retorted with bite and was instantly filled with remorse. "Gabe, I'm SO sorry!!!! See what I mean about my anger, I just lashed out at the hand that's saving me."

"Tia, I'm tougher and more resilient than you think, too. Let's make our exit and get one of those popsicles that are awaiting us back on the boat."

They stood, walked toward the exit with their back to Tia's family. Reaching the door, Tia, tugged on his arm and turned..."just one more peek. For me, Gabe, this was a gift...fireworks a day early."

I'll say, he thought to himself.

Her eyes reached out for one last glance and at just that moment Lina turned in their direction. Tia's heart was pumping overtime as she made herself casually turn and walk through the exit.

Gabe held on to her hand the short ride back to the marina, not offering any words. For her it may have been a gift; for him it was just too close a call, knowing that a surprise confrontation with her lil' sparklers, as she called them, could have set off a family wildfire. It was the last thing that she, Rory or those kids needed at this point.

Back on the boat, he settled her on deck nestled atop an air mattress he'd found below, with pillows and a throw to keep her warmer. Then he went below to get her the promised Popsicle and himself a beer. He really needed something stronger. At the same time he wanted to keep his wits about him. She looked so vacant and desolate.

He put the Josh Groban disc in the boom box, lay down beside her, and gently took her hand once again. Slowly he began rubbing his thumb over her palm, not saying a word, just letting the boat rock them.

Gazing up at the night sky, he hoped there was a God up there and prayed He would be kind. When he looked over Tia was asleep. Softly he brought her fingers to his lips.

Subj: Firecrackers
07/23/02
To: linesbylina
From: Tiara@netsong
    Hey...how's the heat? Thanks for the pictures you e-mailed of the kids taken by your pool when they visited over the 4th!!!!! My mind must really be fuzzy 'cause I just don't recall you e-mailing that they were going to visit you. Meg looked so grown up in that bathing suit...I was semi-shocked that Rory let his little girl get something so high cut! The photo of Sam clowning on the diving board made me laugh out loud...then I cried! However, both are printed prize possessions and keep me motivated. So far, so good, on my end...I've lost six pounds and have no gray hair. Then again, I'm practically hairless everywhere which saves on crème rinse and shaving cream for the legs! Laugh Lina....if I can try, so can you! Please don't worry if you don't hear from me for a while...they said I might have more of a reaction to the next couple of treatments because of the buildup within my system...so I may not be computer compatible for a while.
    You didn't mention Rory and how he was doing? Believe it or not, I care about him even though I'm not in love with him any more. The distance or the disease has shrunk my anger which was a nasty tumor in itself...has he thought at all about following up on the divorce?
    Lina, I also have a small request....Are you groaning, saying 'my gosh, another one?'
    This is just a brainstorm. Use your own good judgment. Do you think you could call the counselor, tell her you and I have been in touch via e-mail only and ask whether or not she thinks it would be a good idea for me to contact the children

in this way by e-mail? I have a long way to go in this treatment plan, yet I don't want to set them back in their own progress if she thinks the idea is just totally selfish on my part.

Love,
me

P.S. By the way, I think it's great you and Rod are finally looking at beach property on the bay side in Galveston, right? Not Kemah?

7/28/02
Subj: Contact
From: linesbylina
To: Tiara@netsong.com

Tia,
*   It's hard to picture you with no hair...you always took such pride in your tresses...I remember the henna in it last winter when you were lying by our pool that spring kissed day last February. Truly, I admire your sense of humor or your efforts at it for my sake. Speaking of last winter, did I tell you we took Rory and the kids to Kemah when they were here? We ate at a restaurant right next to Joe's Crabshack, where we took you. In fact that's where we thought the kids would prefer eating yet the line was too long and your son who was starving (always seems to be starving)! It was weird...once I looked over that way and actually thought I saw someone who looked like you. Then I told myself that it was probably my imagination mixing up last winter with wanting to see you now. Sam didn't get lucky with gull 'splat.' One did nab some of his fries, which he thought was hilarious.*
*   On to more serious matters, the day I got your e-mail I left a message for the counselor. She finally called me back Friday. Since then I've been thinking about what she had to*

say. You know counselors...they ride the line, never giving definitive answers. Between the lines, I think she saw positive merit in a brief e-mail to the kids, letting them know you were thinking about them, that you were at whatever stage in your treatment and to be honest in letting them know you had been e-mailing me or at least to copy me on your e-mail to them so they would have an 'unprotected outlet.' By that, she meant that they would naturally be protective of Rory. He's all they've got and right now their allegiance is with him, though they love you. Remember, my friend, he stayed—you left.

Speaking of Rory, over the weekend they were here and since then I've tried talking to him about moving forward and breaking the 'legal' ties with you. He feels that would just hurt the kids more at this point. He has mentioned this one client a couple of times that's a single mom of a six-year old boy. I'm not sure if there is a spark there or not. Nevertheless, Tia, he just needs more time. You're going to have to let tomorrow take care of itself on this one.

Love,
me

Subject: Phone Home
8/1/02
To: Megmail, Samtheham
cc: linesbylina
From: Tiara@netsong.com

Hi Kids!
Please do not hit delete!!!! I know you might want to make this disappear just the way I disappeared, but please don't. I love you so much and have missed you every second of my time away. I'm copying Aunt Lina on this in case you want to talk to her about it. You can say anything to her and you

know she understands. You are free to show this to Gramma and Gramps, Daddy or whoever.

The folks at the hospital I visit each week are taking very good care of me and so far the treatment is going according to schedule...that's not to give you false hope that I'm all well yet. I have a long way to go and am trying one day at a time.

Did Dad take you to see the re-release of E.T.? When I went to the movies to see it and he said "Phone home," it seemed like a sign that I should write to you, which I hope doesn't make you too sad. Actually, I kinda look like E.T....all eyes and no hair!

If you feel like writing me back, I'd love hearing about what you've been up to during your summer. Each day I play a game imagining what you've done. I may not be able to answer right away as I'm going in for another big treatment in just a few days. After each one, I'm a zombie and spend a lot of time sleeping, eating crackers and just taking it slow.

How did the summer baseball league go? Meg, did Dad sign you up for that quilting camp you wanted to attend?

With all my heart...that is always with you!
Love,
Mom

Subject: Phone Home
8/1/02
From: linesbylina
To: Tiara@netsong.com

Wow...you did it! Please be prepared for whatever reactions you get and don't let anything they say throw you off the course. Remember they are KIDS... ...

Love,

lisa glenn

me

Subj: Phonehome
8/1/02
From: Samtheham
To: Tiara@netsong.com

Mom!!!!

I am so glad you wrote us and I am glad you are okay. I really miss you and we pray for you every night at dinner. I don't think I'm going to tell Dad you e-mailed yet. Meg might not answer your e-mail right away. She's mad on the outside but I know she still really cares. I saw her crumple your e-mail and slam the door to her room, then I heard her crying.

We went to visit Aunt Lina and Uncle Rod in Texas over July 4th. The pool in their backyard is so awesome. There was even a live alligator in the lake behind their house. ET was weird. It's neat the movie made you write us. Our team finished third place and I hit a double in the playoff game. I wish you had been there to see it! Meg decided she didn't want to go to the quilting camp after all. I think she's thinking about trying out for the crew team.

Love you Mom,
Sam

Subj: Phonehome
8/3/02
From: Megmail
To: linesbylina

Dear Aunt Lina,

As you know Mom wrote us. I know she's your very best friend but HOW DARE SHE?

I'm not writing her back!!! Does she think she can just waltz in and out of our lives like a revolving door? Sam was really happy, but we both agreed not to tell Dad right now or our grandparents. I may tell Gramma sometime when we're alone—not yet. Aunt Lina, I know my parents had problems before all this happened with Mom and feel confused about them. Half the kids in my class have parents that are divorced, but that doesn't make thinking about it any easier. All I know is that Dad seems to be doing better than a couple of months ago. He had a client of his over to dinner one night with her little boy, who was okay, I guess. She didn't try to win us over or anything and her kid was okay. As for Mom, I want her to get well, but right now I am still so ANGRY with her for just leaving us. I just can't trust myself to not call her a bitch! Sorry, Aunt Lina…I just had to get it out, and remember your promise to keep my stuff CONFIDENTIAL.

Love,
Meg

Subj: Growing Pains
8/4/02
From: linesbylina
To: Megmail
BCC: (Tiara@netsong.com)

Meg,

Sweetheart, I am so glad you wrote and your words just show how grown up you've become. Your mom loves you…however, that doesn't change the fact that you have every right to what you're feeling. You're on the mark about not writing her back until you can do so without saying things you might regret.

Your mom always teased me about wearing my 'rose colored glasses,' yet I can tell that you don't own a pair. Remember your parents' relationship is NOT your responsibility though it may not be a bad idea to let your dad know that you understand.

Hang in there! Write or call me (collect) any time! It's always a treat when I see Megmail on my screen. In the meantime I'm going to scan in this essay on 'The Seed of the Jack Pine' that your mom copied out of a book of essays by a Dr. Howard Thurman and mailed me back in 1982 when your birth mother Helena was so terribly ill and we were all so confused. I remember thinking then that the essay was on page 82 and it was 1982. Even reading it twenty years later, it made me think of that time, and of 9/11 and of now. Print it out, read it, and think about it.

Love and Hugs,
Aunt Lina

Download

The Seed of the Jack Pine

In response to a letter of inquiry addressed to a Canadian forester concerning the Jack Pine which abounds in British Columbia, the following statement was received: "Essentially, you are correct when you say the Jack Pine cones require artificial heat to release the seed from the cone. The cones often remain closed for years, the seeds retaining their viability. In the interior of the province, the cones which have dropped to the ground will open at least partly with the help of the sun's reflected heat. However, establishment of the majority of our Jack Pine stands has undoubtedly been established following forest fires. Seldom do the cones release their seed while on the tree.

The seed of the Jack Pine will not be given up by the cone unless the cone itself is subjected to sustained and concentrated heat. The forest fire sweeps all before it and there remain but the charred reminders of a former growth and a former beauty. It is then in the midst of the ashes that the secret of the cone is exposed. The tender seed then finds stirring of life deep within itself and what is deepest in the seed reaches out to what is deepest in the life-the result? A tender shoot, gentle roots, until, at last, there stands straight against the sky the majestic glory of the Jack Pine.

It is not too far afield to suggest that there are things deep within the human spirit that are firmly imbedded, dormant, latent and inactive. These things are always positive, even though they may be destructive rather than creative. But there they remain until our lives are swept by the forest fire: human depravity or some moment of agony in which the whole country or nation may be involved. The experience releases something that has been locked up within all through the years. If it be something that calls to the deepest things in life, we may, like the Jack Pine, grow tall and straight against the sky.

Subj: Jack Pine
8/13/03
From Tiara@netsong.com
To: linesbylina

Lina,
*   Thank you for blind copying me on the reply you sent Meg...I was shocked you still had that clipping about the Jack Pine...you who clean out everything on a regular basis and who tease me about being the packrat?!!!!*
*   After all these years, I still felt the power of those words and know I'm the one now undergoing the sustained and concentrated heat of a forest fire and in some ways, my Meg is too. I'm so sorry my body lit the match and my disappearance fueled the fires at least for my dear sweet Meg.*

Subj: You missed the Point
8/14/03
From: linesbylina
To: Tiara@netsong.com

Tia,
*   You missed the point...My friend I am so sorry you have to undergo this heat, if you will, and you know I'm hurting right along with you about Meg, as if she were one of my own girls. However, the point of this story is that it sometimes takes an outside force to open us to what's inside of ourselves that*

is better for us and the universe. You've already admitted that your anger at Rory is growing less and that you've played with ideas for that crazy story you've always wanted to put to paper including every fantasy you've ever had. Let this time be your 'shaman desert' as that psychic once told me...let it be a time of healing and of rejuvenation for you and for your daughter. Remember, she is dealing with more than just your illness...she is dealing with the illness of her birth mother and a mountain of other fears that adolescence carries.

Love you,
me

Popsicles

Subj: Popsicles
8/23/02
From: Tiara@netsong
To: Lines by Lina

Lina,

Thanks for all your e-mails the past ten days or so and for all the cherished updates on my kiddos and what's happening in their lives. I print each one and read it over and over. ...Right after the last treatment it seemed all I did was sleep. Even after a week the anti nausea meds just zapped me and/or my concentration level...that's why I haven't written.

Today I was feeling sorry for myself as I went for another treatment and was allowing myself a real pity party. By the time I walked past the third very frail person in either a wheel chair or a bed, who was hooked up to an IV or had radiation war paint, I said, "Ok God, I get the message!" It may seem horrible to me, but in the scheme of things, I am not doing so bad! Can't really put into words the suspended non-energetic state that I exist within right now. It's a real mind challenge to stay motivated. I am sleeping about 12-13 hours a night, taking naps when I can. It is hard to allow myself to sleep so much. The doctors and nurses say it's normal and what I need right now, yet it feels like that is all I do!...no complaints though, cause at least I'm still here! Lina, I need to share something with you.

This summer Gabe surprised me with a visit. When he first appeared, all I could think was how terrible I looked.

86

However, if he was shocked, he hid it well and told me I was entitled to my 'unique' look. He was so thoughtful, bringing me easy on the stomach goodies he had actually researched, including Margarita flavored Popsicles, as well as flowers to include your personal favorite, sunflowers! It was such a treat having an actual conversation with someone other than sweet Ann, my co-worker, (yes I have a tiny part time job), hospital staff or myself. We talked the gamut of what was going on in our lives.

While I try hard not to let myself think too much about the distant future, if I am healed, I do see life now minus Rory. In the vacuum of my think-tank life these days, I often wonder what held us together more...Catholic upbringing or being slaves to the almighty dollar... that sounds so awful.

Lina, I understand Meg's perspective. When I write Sam and her next I'm going to let her know that I understand.

By the way, Gabe also brought me his laptop. He said he didn't use it much which I'm not sure if I believe. He now has me now hooked up from my digs. So when I can't sleep at night, I can at least play with putting some words together on my book idea that I can 'save' and reread...that is when my concentration is visiting me.

Hey, how is having your oldest son back at home again??? Did your 'baby' go back to school yet?

Love,
me

8/23/02
Subj: Me again
To: Samtheham, Megmail
cc: linesbylina
From:Tiara@netsong

Hi You Two!

    Sam, thanks for e-mailing me and being so grown up in understanding why I felt I had to get away. Your note was like getting a present; one I'll treasurer forever!

    Also thanks for sharing with me the excitement of your double in the playoffs...to coin one of your favorite words, AWESOME!!!!! So glad you had a great time at Aunt Lina's this summer...she sent me a couple of photos on the internet. The one of you on their diving board brought a smile to your mama's heart! Meg, you looked waaaaaaay too grownup in that swimsuit!

    In just a few weeks, school will be starting and hopefully Dad will take you shopping for some new duds!

    Meg I want you to know I completely understand why I haven't heard from you. You're probably both excited and scared about high school, which would be totally normal!

    Remember that first day impressions are important so while I know you want to look 'cool' for your friends, you should also try to be that for your teachers! By that, I mean being on time, having your homework done, etc....you're not a baby anymore...you know the drill. Meg you've always had great grades and Sam you've always tried hard so your Dad and I expect nothing less. Don't even think about using your temporarily motherless status as an excuse to not tow the line!

    Without a doubt, I'll be thinking of you and wishing I was there to get that 'official' first day of school photo even though you both think you're too big for that kinda stuff now.

Much love,
Mom

8/24/02
Subj: Finally!
From: linesbyLina

To: Tiara@netsong.com

Finally, girlfriend!!!
So glad to know you're surviving the drugs! It doesn't take much to recall Helena's lethargy and Gracie's absent-minded non-energy. I don't think either could have very easily handled a teenage household during their chemo so maybe in running away to 'Neverland,' you've done the right thing for self-survival. You gave your kiddos good basics when they were smaller and now, despite the fact that they miss you terribly, they really are doing alright. However, that might not be what you want to hear either...
You know, I would love to be the one giving you some TLC and moral support right now instead of Gabe of the sexy legs! However, I know the rules are that I don't press that point, which is no fair!!!!!
Helena's battle changed my life, so I know your own fight has to have rattled something in that crazy mindset of yours! Tia, I don't think you'll ever really regret trying or sticking your marriage out for as long as you did for the sake of your kids; however, I'm thankful that this reality check (understatement plus!) has opened your eyes. The 'Catholic stigmata' has had its pluses and minuses. I'll always remember Father B's words to me telling me to ask myself if my marriage was simply 'legal' rather than spiritual. He made me think! Indeed, there is something to be said for thought-filled faith versus the blind kind! Call me what you will, yet when I went to confession right after the divorce was final 15 years ago (and I hadn't been in years and not since), the scripture reading the priest gave me as penance—you know: the one about the flood and the rainbow clinched it. Forgiven is how I felt for all my mea culpas. Again, I think this is your time in the shaman desert, as the philosophers say.
Tia, when the worst of this is past, please, please consider coming back, facing the kids and Rory. In fact if you

want my unsolicited opinion, I think you need to make contact with Rory, share your feelings and what's going on.

To answer your questions, the 'baby' went back to school August 21ˢᵗ and it's an adjustment having the grown son back in the nest...very different. Guess it's not yet my time for the empty nest I so dreaded...the good Lord is going to make me beg for it!

Love,
me
P.S. Good luck with any writing efforts you're able to undertake! You go girl! You always were the more creative one.

Subj: Advice
8/24/02
From: Tiara@netsong.com
To: linesbylina

Shock! Two days in a row! Double Shock: good advice Lina. Thanks. Will e-mail Rory... Next week is another big treatment so you may not hear from me for a while again.

I love you....so much.....
me

Subj: White Flag Waving!!!!
8/24/02
From: Tiara@netsong.com
To: Ror7

Bald as a bat, white as a ghost, a bit thinner and doing okay. My prayer is that you are too. You and the kids didn't deserve my disappearing act. At the time I thought I was doing this for Meg, Sam, my family, you. I've come to realize that I did this as much for myself as for all of you. Some days I can barely stand my own reflection so I know I would have hated the one I'd see through the mirror of your collective eyes.

It's time for some honesty. I've been in contact with Lina and the kids via e-mail. Lina was sworn to secrecy under threat of no contact. If the kids haven't mentioned anything, it's because they love and are protecting you. Sam has e-mailed me back and Meg has been silent, which I understand.

Rory, I hope you're moving on. I am. If nothing else, this time has shown us all that we can be apart and be okay. Life's too short and too precious to live it in limbo. Rory, we both deserve to be happy. Sure, Meg and Sam will have some scar tissue yet doesn't everyone of some sort or another. Wasn't it in the last lines of that movie 'Hope Floats' where Sandra Bullock says, "childhood is what we spend the rest of our life getting over."

Despite my efforts to breeze over the pain we've both felt, I ask you to just think about what I've said.

Tia
P.S. Good Luck with the back-to-school shopping!

Subj: Thinkingboutit
8/26/02
From: Ror7
To: Tiara@netsong

Tia,

Asking me to think from your perspective right now is a bit much, although I am really relieved to know you're out there fighting for your life. Can't say I wasn't angry and can't say it doesn't hurt to be the last contacted. I'll keep this short *as I don't trust myself not to say something we both might regret, and remember, 'beauty is in the eye of the beholder.' Your eyes might not be seeing what we would...they never have.*

Rory
P.S. Don't worry about the school shopping...it'll get done and I promise to smile every time they swipe the VISA. The kids have been great.

Running Shoes

Staring out the window of his Belleview condo, Gabe could just barely see a few joggers through the trees on the parkway trail along the Potomac. Self-admittedly looking for a place to relocate and semi-retire, he knew part of himself would always be attached to this place. He liked living near the river and the running path. It had been a beautiful day and right now the temperature was perfect. He should be out there working up a sweat and enjoying the scenery. Maybe he would. Before you knew it, the leaves would be falling. Right now everyone seemed to be taking advantage of this Indian summer evening. He hadn't really exercised since day before yesterday and inwardly prided himself on not having a mid-life tire. It wouldn't hurt to relieve some stress and clear out the cobwebs either.

Walking towards his room to change clothes, the phone rang. Looking at the Caller ID, he could feel his entire body tense up.

"Mr. Gibonni?"

"Yes, this is Gabe Gibonni."

"Sir, this is Emily Hunter. I'm a nurse at the St. Bartholemew's Health Research Center and your name is listed as the emergency contact on the forms for a Ms. Tia Titanni, who has been undergoing treatment here as an outpatient. We admitted Ms. Titanni yesterday due to the fact that her white blood cell count was extremely high and she was extremely weak. Ms. Titanni said she lived alone with no family nearby. Dr. Lauder thought you should be notified and that you might want to pay her a visit."

"Is she going to be okay? Is she alright?"

"Well, sir, you'd really have to speak with the doctor to get more detailed information; however, right now Ms. Titanni is stable. The doctor is contemplating release day after tomorrow pending someone being there to watch over her for a few days until we do a follow-up check and new blood work."

"Ms. Hunter, right? I will make arrangements to fly there sometime early tomorrow. I have a small favor to ask. Please don't let Ms. Titanni know that I'm coming. She's manically independent and this way my arrival will be a surprise. Thanks for calling."

"You're so welcome. I'll note this on her chart for Dr. Hunter and leave the day shift nurse a notation that you'll be arriving to care for Ms. Titanni. She's lucky to have a friend such as yourself. Goodnight Mr. Gibonni."

"Goodnight and thanks again."

"Tia, Tia, Tia what am I gonna do with you, girl?' he said aloud to himself as he hung up the phone.

Somehow, even though he'd managed to file her away for years, she had now gotten under his skin, baggage and all. He wasn't going to fight it any longer. He had plenty of leave, no pressing cases, and she needed him, whether she wanted to admit it or not.

Thinking to himself, he began a mental checklist: call the office, make a reservation, leave a note in his mailbox to stop the mail, pack a few things (he was sure glad he forced himself to do laundry over the weekend!). Now he really did need that run…there was one big dangling matter he felt he should take care of before he left tomorrow and maybe ruminating on the run would help him decide just how to approach the unapproachable.

Coffee and Donuts

Tia wouldn't like this, not one little bit. It was the right thing to do, and whenever possible he liked playing by the rules.

According to her, Rory stopped at the old Waffle Shop for coffee and a donut before heading to work each morning. He hoped he was there now and alone. Tackling this sensitive subject in a public place was probably a bit underhanded, yet at the same time he hoped it would keep passions to a reasonable level.

Walking past the smoking section, he spotted him in a booth reading the paper. Maybe luck was on his side at least, although he couldn't help but notice that Rory looked so gray and much too thin.

"Rory."

Rising up from the booth, Rory smiled with his eyes, "Gabe! Hey, Man, Great to see you! Tia told me she ran into you in Texas this past winter. We don't see you for ages and now we've both run into you the same year."

"Yeah, well...Rory, this isn't a coincidence. There's something I need to talk to you about. Mind if I sit down? Thanks."

"Sure, sit, I don't have long though, before I have to leave to get to work."

"Whew...Where to begin. Rory, please just hear me out before you throw any punches across this booth."

"Gabe, remember...it's me Rory, the pacifist. You're the one who packs a gun."

"Hold up, hear me out and then we'll see how peaceful you feel. When Tia and I ran into each other in Kemah last year, did she tell you we had dinner and did a lot of catching up?"

"Oh, yeah...she said she really enjoyed seeing you and told me how she scared the hell out of Lina when she got up from lunch to approach some stranger." Rory smiled, remembering how animated she had been telling him that story. He also recalled wishing he could bring that kind of excited look to her eyes.

Gabe laughed. "Yes, well that's Tia; always adding drama to a moment."

"More than you know, ole buddy," replied Rory.

"No, Rory. That's the point. I do know about Tia's illness. Let me back up."

"I'm confused. What's this got to do with you?" said Rory with a frown.

Rory sat there in undisguised disbelief as Gabe relayed Tia's situation and his role over the past few months. Only the look in his eyes, the flex in his jutting jaw, and the clenching and unclenching of his fingers registering to Gabe the range of betrayal and anger he must be feeling.

"You know where she is?"

"Yes, I do, though I made a promise to her that I wouldn't divulge either her identity or her location. I'm sorry."

"Gabe, then why in the hell are you here?" Rory asked barely keeping his Irish temper under a lid.

"Look, Rory. I know this is tough. She's your wife and she left you with the kids and a big hole. From talking to her last winter it seemed the situation between the two of you was not the best and hasn't been for a while. Believe me, I was really sorry to hear that."

"Cut to the chase, Gabe!"

"The hospital called me last night advising me she'd been admitted because of an infection."

"Okay, back up," Rory's voice menaced a little too loudly for Gabe's public comfort level. "I'm still in the dark here as to why she chose to confide in you. Why *you* know where she is and why the hospital called *you*??? Is there or was something going on between the two of you that I am totally missing here?"

"You're not missing a thing, Rory. When you two lived in the same apartment complex as I did years ago, I'll admit that I thought you were a damn lucky guy to have someone like her. I've always admired her spunk. Last winter when we ran into each other, it was just great to see her and catch up…that was it! Why did she choose me? I think it's because I was NOT someone from her inner sanctum and she wanted someone she could trust and who could be objective in their support."

"Well, imagine that," Rory said, rolling his eyes and dripping with sarcasm. "She doesn't trust me! Everyone knows that! I never do anything right or to her standard of satisfaction, from how I wipe down the kitchen counters to how I help the kids with homework. Just tell her highness that we're doing just fine on our own. The house hasn't fallen down and the kids aren't flunking a thing. So, Gabe, maybe among my other unaccomplished traits I'm just dense. At the risk of repeating myself, why in the hell are you telling me all this now?"

"Rory, I'm taking off today to go take care of her and I just thought it was right that you know. Tia doesn't even know it yet. In fact, I told the head nurse not to tell her I was coming. She's so damned independent. I visited her about a month or six weeks ago, and even then she looked like a good breeze would knock her over. Rory, she doesn't look the same; she has that war refugee look, like someone battling cancer and she is extremely weak if you can imagine Tia being that."

Rory put his head in his hands.

Gabe felt like a first class ball-buster.

"Gabe, if you came here to get my blessing, I think that's a bit of a reach, although at some level I know I should feel grateful you are willing to be there for Tia. To tell you the truth though, man, everything you've just told me just brings all the anger inside of me back to the surface. I feel like a morphing monster."

"You could be right. Maybe in some misguided way I did come here for your blessing under the guise of being up front. I just know that she needs someone now. I've got the leave to use, no family of my own, and I truly care about Tia, maybe more than I want to admit to you, she or even myself."

Rory looked Gabe straight in the eye and with a warning edge in his voice said "I am not ready for that discussion at the moment no matter what kind of problems Tia and I have."

"Gabe, I've got to get to work. Just so you know, I am going to tell my kids, her family and Lina that you are going there, whereever there is, to be with Tia for a while. Though they may not understand this any better than I do at this moment, I know it will give them some sense of comfort to know that she is not totally alone. I also know that I'm going to probably walk around the rest of the day like I've dreamt this conversation."

Rory stood to leave.

"This isn't easy on any of us," said Gabe. He wanted to offer his hand yet knew if he were in Rory's shoes, he'd leave it dangling, so thought better of it, surprised that he could even think clearly at all at this point.

"No, it's no picnic for anyone," Rory mumbled as he walked out without looking back. He should be punching this guy's lights out. In his gut he knew none of this was Gabe's fault.

Hospital Helper

It really was true and probably couldn't be helped. Hospitals had their own scent and something about them just gave one the heebie-jeebies. Perhaps the only exception was going to visit a maternity ward and seeing those fresh newborns behind the glass. Even then you realized that the floor above you or the floor below could house some very sick folks.

It was a little after 11: 30 a.m. and he was thankful that the airport was only about a half hour from the medical center where St. Bartholomew's was centered.

Lord knows how Tia was going to react when he walked through the door, or about his plan to be the one to take her back to the boat. He wasn't going to mention the length of his stay until he got her settled and she'd had a good rest. And for sure he wasn't going to tell her about his talk with Rory til she had her strength back. The trip from the hospital itself was probably going to wear her out.

Taking the elevator up to the 7th floor he could feel his pulse accelerating. He was a grown man, an FBI Agent who had seen corpses, mutilated bodies, crime victims and worse. The difference was they were 'subjects.' Thank God, his family had not suffered any run-ins with disease. Gabe only hoped he'd have the wherewithal and the courage to be what Tia needed right now. For sure, he was winging it.

Checking in at the nurse's station, he identified himself and was told to wait. Fortunately he did not have to wait long.

"Mr. Gibonni?"

"Yes," he said, standing.

"How do you do? Please sit down. I'm Milagros Santera and am the charge nurse. Per the notation in Ms. Titanni's chart by Nurse Hunter last evening, Dr. Lauder is releasing her to your care. We need you to sign this release and initial the page of instructions. Ms. Titanni needs to return in a week to have her medi port cleaned as she does each week; however, we'd like to show you how to do the syringe cleaning. We suspect the infection she came down with has to do with her sleeping through or forgetting to run the fluids through the medi port tubes as she must daily." The nurse paused for a moment to give him time to register the information she had just given him.

"Mr. Gibonni, would you be willing to learn this technique as a backup in case Ms. Titanni is not able to do this for herself?"

Gabe swallowed, "Yes, of course." (What had he let himself in for? He didn't even know she had a shunt. He should have realized.)

"Just follow me, sir. This won't hurt at all," the nurse said with a fun-filled wink.

After forty-five minutes of learning sterile techniques that he could have sworn were more harrowing than bomb disarming, he rolled down his sleeves and noticed his hands were no longer sweating. Really, it wasn't that bad. He just didn't want to screw up. Poor Tia, there were so many things to remember…times to take medications, cleaning that 'thing,' feeling lousy, and having no one to simply be there for her. From now on, things were going to be different, and after that class he wasn't about to put up with any of her sass!

He asked the nurse to let her know she had a visitor, gave her a few minutes and now he was walking in. Why did he feel like he was walking into a sniper's lair?

Walking toward her bed, Gabe placed a gentle kiss on her forehead.

"Tst, Tst, Tia…a little bird told me you've been a very bad patient. They only send for the FBI in circumstances such as this when the subject has crossed state lines, or when they are armed and dangerous. You have crossed state lines. You have arms and you are definitely dangerous to yourself."

Oh, here he was again, her proverbial white knight and though she shouldn't be, she told herself, she was indeed glad to set her makeup-less eyes on him.

"Gabe, you need a bit of work before you set up a gig as a standup comic. So! Which one of the white coats called you???"

Despite the hospital pallor, the smile in her eyes called to him. He was so glad to see some spark and knew that behind it someway, somehow, someday...there would be fireworks out of this lady once again.

"Tia, it doesn't matter who called. I have the distinct honor of being the emergency contact on your paperwork, and the fact is you weren't going to be allowed to spring this joint without an armed guard. I volunteered. So no arguments, okay?"

"Do I have any choice in the matter?"

"None."

"So when do we leave?" she asked like a little kid waiting for a big moment.

"When your wheels arrive for the ride down and you're ready."

Slowly she swung her legs over the side of the bed. She was dressed in some capris and a long t-shirt. Sitting up she felt a bit dizzy and closed her eyes. Gabe took a step closer. She leaned her head against his chest.

"I'm glad you're here."

"Me, too," he replied. Putting his arms gently around her he laid a kiss atop her head so light Tia thought she imagined it; given with such restrained emotion from his world, which suddenly seemed to be rocking.

9/10/02
Subject: From Mom in Neverland
To:Samtheman
From:Tiara@netsong.com

Hi Sam and Meg!
Sorry I've been out of touch...I had a bit of a relapse from

some of the treatments and was under the covers longer than what's normal even for my not-normal life right now; however, I thought about you all the time and wondered how your first week of classes went? What teachers you liked and if you got all the school supplies you needed. Mom Stuff I guess, yet I know Dad is doing a terrific job.

Sam, are you going to play lacrosse this Fall? Meg, did you decide if you were going to go out for crew?

Please know I love you and am thinking of you and keeping visions of you two as my finish line medal..........

All my love,
Mom

Still Waters

Standing in the middle of the cozy, yet compact, seaside bungalow, he told himself it was a good investment. He wasn't being impulsive. Hell, he had been dragging his feet on a much needed change of direction because there really had been no big hurry, believing the winds of fate would grab his attention when the time was right. (And HOW!!). He wasn't doing this for Tia. After all, that's why he had traveled here back in February before Pandora's box was opened— to look at property along the water. Jack said it was a great place to kick back, even retire. He loved the Chesapeake, yet he wanted the warmth of the sun a good bit of the year to boat and golf and yes, even dabble with his paint brushes again...

Three days ago when he brought Tia back from the hospital, carrying her down the ladder into the cabin...well, it wasn't easy. Not a negative word or complaint had slipped from her mouth, yet he could see the white lines of pain as he had set her down.

The very next day while she was sleeping, he called the realtor he had worked with during the winter and with whom he had been in weekly contact via e-mail. Chuckling to himself, he remembered the stunned silence on the other end of the line when he told her he was ready, wanted something that he could at least rent with the option to buy in the next 24 hours and that he had cash in the bank to back up his words.

Now, here he was after all these years of bachelor living in that cracker box condo, a landowner on the Gulf. He mentally hummed, yet just couldn't help smiling to himself, like some big sap. The investor in him knew he'd really lucked out with this small geometric gem...what was the word those fancy-pants decorators used, rustic...that's it. Sure it needed some paint, some weatherproofing, yet it was sound, and it was HIS! He couldn't wait to surprise Tia…he had begun bringing things from the boat over slowly, not that there was that much.

The beds he ordered by phone would be arriving any minute and the sofa was supposed to arrive soon, also. After the deliveries he would go back to the boat, check on her and then, time allowing, he would go get some bedding, and other practical necessities. Tia's friend, Ann, from the shop had been a lifesaver in helping him select things for Tia's room. If all went according to plan and she was feeling up to it, tomorrow he would tell her they were going for a nice relaxing ride. The dry land destination would be a real surprise.

Lifting the Fog

9/07/02
Subject: Slow but Sure
From: Tiara@netsong.com
To: linesbylina

Hello out there...
Hope all is well and I'm sorry if you've been worried. It's a long story and to be blunt I just don't have it in me right now to go into all the details. In fact, I detest this no energy feeling that makes my life feel so out of control. Gabe is here with me now after he got an SOS from the white coats that I needed some up close care following an infection (don't worry-more-or-less okay, now). He's running an errand at the moment and actually it's the first day since I was released from the hospital that I even feel like sitting upright. I did send Sam and Meg a short note too.

He has been amazing and I have to admit that it's been a blessing, mixed in some ways, to have him here, waiting on me hand and foot, or should I say 'hand and food.' It made me think of how Helena's mom would bring her those daily food plates and how we teased her about being the 'kitchen police.' Remember—she pretended to be chatting or doing some small task, when really she was watching with eyes in the back of her head to make sure Helena ate a good portion of what was on that plate or at least made a stab at it. Gabe is her kitchen clone!

Just please call or e-mail Rory and the kids to let them know I am surviving these body poisons that are hopefully killing the bad cells as well as some of the good ones along the way. Gabe said it's like a bad crime scene where innocent victims get hurt as the bad guys are getting caught!

Love you,
me
9/13/02
Subj: Personal care
From: linesbylina
To: Tiara@netsong.com

Tia,

Hope this won't be a shock to your system, yet did your 'friend' Gabe tell you he paid Rory a visit at the Waffle Shop the morning he left to play nurse????? Sorry!!! Didn't mean that to sound sarcastic. Needless to say it caused Rory an emotional roller coaster ride for a couple of days. To be honest, the fact that you have Gabe listed on your medical forms sent me down a slide of my own. (Yeah, I know, it's all about me!). Rory, however, is making progress, and before he talked to your family or the kids, he did meet with the counselor. He's finally learning, I think, that there is no shame in getting some help from an objective third party. He's also reaching out more in general, which shows he's making changes within himself for himself.

Tia, I know it's challenging for you to have positive feelings about Rory, yet he dealt with a male he hasn't seen for years coming up to him out of the blue one morning, telling him he was going to take care of the wife whose whereabouts he knows not! When he spoke to your kids and family he very gently (actually, he should get an academy award!!!) told them that an old mutual friend had gone to take care of you after a really bad spell, explaining this person could be more objective (???) That word keeps popping up and maybe it's been needed for the past decade or more! He also planted the seed with Meg and Sam that you might live apart when you get well, saying this time apart had shown you both how unhappy you were together. He made it very clear it had nothing to do with them

You know I love you, sister-friend, yet I hope you realize that while you've been battling for your life against disease, he's been defending and maintaining the home front. I'm not being 'his' cheerleader or anything else. You've always wanted him to take more responsibility and though your illness forced his hand, he has stepped to the plate...

Will do as you asked and let the family know how you are.

On a totally female level, I'd like to know what's going through that head and heart of yours having that hunk of hero there as your male nurse?????? Is it just the meds and/or the popsicles that are still giving you chills these days????

Love,
me

Surprise, Surprise!

Despite the kerchief across her eyes and Gabe's pirate tactics, she was enjoying this jaunt immensely. It felt good to be out in the fresh sea scented air, taking a ride just like a normal person. She could almost picture the white capped surf and the reeds along the water swaying in the breeze. In fact, with the hardtop off the Jeep, she felt like a kid again and knew Sam would love riding in this high tech dune buggy. Meg, on the other hand would be worrying about her hair while thinking inwardly this was too-something!

So much had been going through her head these past few days while she was waiting she was, 'confined to quarters,' as Gabe put it. When she'd first confronted him about his true confession to Rory, he didn't go defensive and he didn't apologize, matter-of-factly pointing out that Rory had a right to know that another man was going to be living and caring for his wife. In fact, seen through her new cancer- enhanced vision, she was having an epiphany of sorts about Rory and life in general. Within her heart, she knew they were not a couple 'God joined,' yet rather both victims to some degree of the *Ozzie and Harriet, Donna Reed, Leave it to Beaver, Brady Bunch* era that sent out the signal that one needed only to be married to be happy and complete. Those shows didn't make your choices, yet they were the veritable Eve holding out the apple of 'happily ever after' that she and so many of her generation had bit into before they found out about the rotten spots. Unfortunately, those shows didn't go into the intricacies of marriage and relationships in the way of today TV.

"C'mon, Gabe, where are we going? Can I take this silly blindfold off?"

"Patience, woman! I guess you are feeling better since you're being rather feisty this morning. Just sit back, relax and listen to this tape. It won't be long."

"Feisty?" Tia's voice escalated a notch or two…"you think *this* is feisty? Mister, you just don't know how lucky you are that you were off the boat when I first read that e-mail from Lina yesterday about you being such an 'honest Abe' with Rory before coming here. If you only knew how fortunate you were that I had a chance to breathe and calm down. I so wanted to throw the kettle at you and ask questions later."

"Oh," he smirked, "What questions?"

"Like whether you thought you were some sort of chivalrous Texas Ranger cum shrink now, instead of an aging FBI agent."

"Aging FBI Agent?!!!! You really are a lil she-cat this morning aren't you? Just tuck away those claws or soon you'll be regretting those catty words. My last name isn't Gibonni for nothing, ya know"

"What are you talking about now?"

"Gibbronis is an Italian slang term which is the same as 'cojones' in Spanish and 'balls' in English, so just keep that in mind when you're dealing with me, lady."

"Something tells me I'm never going to be able to forget or even top that, tough guy," laughed Tia.

Her body could feel the Jeep turn and heard the crunch of gravel under the wheels. The salt air smells were getting stronger. He must be taking her to the beach. They came to a stop; she heard his door slam and seconds later, hers was opened…

"Hold on and follow me, woman," Gabe said with a definite up note in his voice.

"Against my better judgment," she quipped, as she placed her hand in his.

Walking slowly, she could hear him pull out a key and open up a door.

Gently, he led her over a threshold and then turned her…she could feel his hands untying the goofy black blindfold!

"Ohhhhh," escaped her mouth immediately. In front of her eyes was a living seascape through a bowed bay window…it looked like something out of a coffee table book…

"Welcome to our new digs!"

Her eyes filled as she turned and spread her arms with a look that said more than just how, when, what is this?????

"Come on, lady, don't look so non-plussed! Even though you've lost all that weight you wanted to, it's not easy carrying you down that ladder to the galley and after all, THIS is the reason I originally was checking out Texas coastline property last winter! It would be my distinct pleasure to give you the grand tour, Madame," raising his dark brows Clark Gable style and proffering a forearm...

"Lead away," she said, wrapping her arm through his. Her eyes were already taking in every detail.

"As you can see to the right, we have a cozy yet efficient little kitchen. Compared to the on-board galley it looked downright large. Notice the vintage blue and white tile work and the cobalt blue porcelain sink, which I scrubbed to it's gleaming shine myself. Be sure you don't overlook the ole' Frigidare either. See the gold crown at the top...Remember when they used to give away iceboxes on that old *Queen for a Day* show, like it was every homemakers dream?" remarked Gabe.

"Different model woman back then too," retorted Tia feeling good enough not to let a sharp line go by. "In those post-war, baby-boomer growing up years, I guess our moms were happy with anything that made life easier. They probably weren't as high maintenance as the middle class mamas of today who'd probably prefer a facial, a day at the spa or a trip to the Bahamas! What I want to know is how you managed this real estate miracle so fast and without my knowing a thing?"

"All it takes is cash, cold hard cash, baby," he replied now using a Bogart accent. More seriously, "And remember, I've had several real estate offices checking out property for quite awhile, as well as using some of my own 'aging FBI' investigative techniques working on this case for quite a while."

"Gabe, it's almost too perfect...even the chipped paint and weathering looks good, like something out of a design magazine."

"You ain't seen nothing yet, sweetheart," he continued in his Bogie voice. "Down this hall to the left we have your classic retro bathing facility complete with more vintage tile and a claw foot tub. The folks who previously owned this place did a really great job renovating, especially with their eye for detail...look at those fixtures."

"Gabe, you're sounding like the guy on that *Home Improvement* show now."

" Nah...I'm just in awe of folks who know how to do a job well in the purist sense. Now let me lead you to your suite, such as it is," he said opening the door to the next room.

"Oh, the quilt is beautiful!!! Where did you find this!" exclaimed Tia.

It was a patchwork of soft blues, misty greens, mellow yellows, some raspberry pink and other soft colors. On the floor beside it was a rag rug of the same tones that set off the gleam in the hardwood floor.

"Hey, a guy can't give away all his sources and as you can see there's no real furniture to speak of, though, I will give your friend Ann at the shop the credit for sending me to a certain shop for the quilt and rug. I figured when you were stronger we could take a road trip and check out some antiques from the Wild West."

"Talk about wild, it feels like I've fallen through the looking glass."

Taking her wrist and leading her back down the hall, past his own room, back through the open living-dining room, he led her out towards the screen porch.

"You've got to be getting tired and probably should get off your feet for a bit. Remember, this is your first outing in over a week. However, before you take your mid-day siesta, I have one other little surprise just for you."

To the left, hanging from the rafters was a new porch swing with one yellow rose upon it and a card. She walked over, gingerly sat down and opened the card a bit nervously. Then, as her eyes skimmed over it, she suddenly burst out laughing!

"Whaaaaaaaaaaaat?" he said. "You don't like my poetry?" he asked with a raised eyebrow and his killer grin.

Roll with the punches
Rock with the tide
Tia, my bald-headed buddy,
Your caretaker always, I'll stay at your side!

Celebrate

Tia was at the sink dicing tomatoes for homemade pasta sauce, marveling at how she was enjoying this simple kitchen duty and this beautiful day, though it was hard to believe it was already October and that they'd been in the cottage a month! Back East the leaves would be turning and starting to fall...here it still seemed summerlike. As soon as she saw them for sale, she was going to get a couple of pumpkins for the cottage. Sam had always been anxious to carve their funny faces...*don't go there* she told herself or you'll just fall in a black hole. Mentally shaking herself, she wondered if they sold gourds in Texas...it would be nice to put a basket full by the fireplace.

It was truly unsettling how well she and Gabe got along and how well they cohabitated together thought Tia. There seemed to be humor at every rough turn to soften the edges and just an easy rhythm in accomplishing the smallest of tasks. With Rory there had been tension in every step, even in the beginning, as well as a cloud of frustration at his seemingly lackadaisical approach to every task. She no longer looked in the mirror of her mind's eye and saw a witch-bitch. She was softer and maybe her entire perspective had changed. Was it the weight of a ball-n-chain marriage cut loose that had transformed her or was it realizing that certain things weren't as important as they once seemed?

"Since you're feeling pretty good today, what do you say we dine out tonight along the boardwalk? I feel like celebrating!"

"Oh, and what pray tell are we celebrating?"

"Let's see, I think we've got a lot to celebrate! Number one, your doctor said only four more treatments, which means you'll be finished right around the Christmas holidays. Number two, my early retirement offer from the Bureau, which means I can set up the private investigative business I've been thinking about for my new semi-retired life; and number three, your giant step in calling Rory the other night so the two of you could actually talk person to person, to get some things settled so you can both move forward."

He was absolutely right (again!), Tia thought. We do have a lot to celebrate. She knew that when Rory told her he was ready to make their separation legal, amazingly with no real bitterness in his voice, it seemed as if a huge boulder had been lifted from her. They decided together that she would call the family on Thanksgiving Day just to reintroduce her voice; and then Rory said he would like to break the news to Meg and Sam that Saturday after as it would give the three of them the weekend to talk through any immediate fall-out. It was ironic that they had come to this crucial life crossing together in more peace than they had in their actual marriage, which somehow said it all. A priest once told her that when you have peace in your heart over a decision, you knew it was right.

"Earth to Tia, Earth to Tia…"

"Sorry! My mind was on one its little trips…you should be used to that by now."

"Well, if you're back, what do you think about going out?"

"Sounds like a plan," said Tia, "And I'll put a reserve on my energy so that I won't poop out on you at sunset! We can have the pasta tomorrow. Next week after my treatment I'll be good for nothing."

"Okay then! I'll do KP and you go take a long soak in the tub in some of that herbal stuff that's supposed to be good for relaxation. We'll go around 6:00 p.m. and watch the boats come in."

Giving his shoulder a squeeze as she walked by, "Thanks."

"For what?"

"For reminding me we have a lot to celebrate, that *I* have a lot to celebrate," she said as she walked back to her room, thinking if all went well it wouldn't be long before she could at least think about calling and maybe evening seeing the kids again. She missed everything about her world with them so much… even going over homework, car pools, harping on Sam to put his lacrosse paraphernalia away, and especially most watching Meg debut at crew. When Sam had e-mailed the link to Meg's crew team website and she'd seen how her beautiful daughter had blossomed in just these past few months, she was amazed. Yes, she was even grateful to Rory that he had taken charge and done so well with the children. Perhaps the fault had been hers in expecting him to always offer to help or pitch in, rather than just asking or admitting she needed his support. It seemed the Lord had taught her a valuable lesson in learning that people don't have the opportunity to give, unless someone is willing to receive and that sometimes, receiving is the hardest part!

Fighting Words—
Desperate Measures

"Tia," he called out, as he came through the door. No answer. "She must be resting," he thought. This recent treatment had been a rough one in terms of side affects...Tia hadn't been able to keep much down all week and had been more pale and lethargic than the previous times. While he realized he was used to her look, this was the weakest he had observed her and decided to push his angst away for now.

Gabe figured he'd go ahead and make himself a big sandwich and watch some Sunday afternoon football while Tia finished her nap. It was easier digging into food when she wasn't sitting right there anyway. Like himself, the stereo-typical Italian, Tia loved food, and Gabe knew that despite weight loss perks she missed having an appetite. Maybe he would catch the Redskins on cable. He was hoping that young quarterback would get to throw the ball. Ever since Tia's 'yayas,' as she referred to Lina and Gracie, had gone to Virginia Beach to cheer on Lina's daughter in a Leukemia and Lymphoma Society's Labor Day Weekend Rock'N Roll Half Marathon, fatefully offering a ride to the Washington team's number two quarterback, they had become Redskin groupies; correction, a particular quarterback's groupies!

Gabe and Tia both had gotten such a kick out of their obvious excitement. Thinking the quarterback was simply some young kid with his cousin in the hotel lobby, just trying to navigate their way to the heart of the race like they were, Lina offered them a ride in the cab they'd called. Making introductions in the parking lot of the Cavalier and learning Lina was living in Houston, he told them he had been living in the neighboring city of New Orleans, working with inner city kids. Gracie, another forthright Sagittarian, asked why he was now living in Virginia and he 'fessed up to the fact that he was playing football for the Redskins. Lina had attached proof positive photos and e-mailed that no one had ever seen a woman rip off a raincoat faster than Gracie, who then put her arm around this pigskin pro and ordered Lina to "hurry it up and capture this "Kodak moment!" Tia's friends had drooled over his gallantry in helping them track down where Lina's daughter would be throughout the race and easing their anxieties about this being her rookie half marathon. Terese, Lina's daughter had finished better than anyone had anticipated and called the event "the greatest non-academic achievement of her life." She had worn Helena and Tia's names on the back of her shirt. What had surprised Tia most was that Lina and Gracie had taken Meg along with them to experience the event. Her obvious pleasure in being treated like one of the women was evident in her glowing smile! Chuckling inwardly, he still was amazed at how much two grown women and one teenager could get out of one guy on a ten-minute cab ride! Now the Virginia Beach troupe was all tuning into Redskin gridiron each week for a glimpse of their personal hero!

Finishing lunch, Gabe felt himself getting sleepy and decided to go horizontal for the rest of the game, knowing there would be a play-by-play report from Lina via e-mail the next morning if 'their' boy took to the field.

Quite a few zzz's later, Gabe woke to a setting sun and chastised himself for sleeping so long...now he'd be up all night! Sitting up and rubbing the sleep from his eyes, he decided it was time to check on Tia.

First he'd heat her some broth with the shaved vegetables he'd put together the day before. She really did need to try and get something down.

Tray in hand, he walked down the hall and slowly opened her door...she was turned away from him on her side. He put the tray down and turned the light on low. Still there was no movement. He gingerly sat down on the side of the bed and felt something under him. It was a piece of paper. He lifted himself an inch and picked it up...

October 4, 2002
From: Megmail
To: Tiara@netsong.com
Subject: Truth

Tia,

  Did you know that in Italian or maybe it's Spanish tia means aunt? You are technically my cousin and legally my guardian, but from now on that's how I've chosen to address you. A real mother wouldn't desert her kids. I am sorry you are sick and I really do hope you get better. At the same time, I feel you didn't give us the chance to be there for you. Some example, yeah right?!

  Maybe it's because you are not my real mother that I can see this all like I'm looking through a window. When I think of you and Dad, I don't think of a couple and I overheard Dad talking with you on the phone, saying he was going to tell us after Thanksgiving that you two were splitting up and that you are living somewhere with an old friend who happens to be a guy. All those life-lessons from your end seem to be all talk. Do as I say, not as I do...you're shacking up! And you definitely got going when the going got tough.

  Don't worry, I don't share all these bitchie thoughts with Sam. Aunt Lina defends you, and I know Dad will too. Despite the way you've ragged on him in the past and how you left him holding the bag with us, he still seems to care. The counselor, Dad, Aunt Lina everyone says to share....and you're really the only one who deserves my black thoughts.

Meg

Whoa...the kid was angry...that's for sure, and who could blame her. Yet, reading this had to be like a kick in the gut to Tia. Gabe only wished there was something, he could do! Unfortunately he knew of nothing that would take away the pain that little poison pen letter had inflicted on Tia.

Putting the paper down, he gently touched Tia's bone thin shoulder. "Tia, wake up." No movement. Slowly he turned her over and still she didn't respond.

"What the hell?" Somewhat panicked, he tried feeling for a pulse. It was weak at best. "Come on, babe." Picking up the phone, he dialed 911. Reassured the ambulance was the way, he then called Tia's doctor who said she'd meet them at the hospital.

Relief...just a swallow away. "Lina, she's going to be fine."

"Gabe, how can you say that with such confidence when four hours ago you called here out of your mind that she wasn't going to pull through."

"Hey, I know I'm supposed to be calm, cool and collected yet this wasn't a crime scene, this was Tia. Her blood pressure had dropped, and I was waiting for the doctor to come out of the examining room. Tia is now stable and the doctor has assured me she's going to be okay. In fact she said that some blood work the lab sent back before this happened looked promising for a change. Lina, what I didn't tell you a couple of hours ago was that when I found Tia she was laying on a rather scathing e-mail from Meg...one that would have broken any mother's heart, much less a mother who is as sick and worn down as she is."

"Oh, God, Gabe...I feel so bad for both of them...Tia and Meg."

"Yeah, I know. Obviously from her missive, Meg overheard Rory talking to Tia a few weeks back telling her that he was going to talk to she and Sam about their separation. It's just not a good situation."

"Gabe, I think it's time for a reality check..."

"Agreed, yet let's get her home from the hospital first...I've got an idea that I'll share with you in more detail...just give me a couple of weeks to get her back in fighting shape."

The Festival of Lights

It was 40 degrees, the day had truly been Christmas cookie cozy with Gabe's fire crackling in the old stone fireplace…she hadn't wanted to ruin the mood by telling him of the decision she had come to now that the doctors had finally told her she was in remission…hopefully for always…yet at least for now. Tomorrow…no, she was not putting this off like Scarlett in *Gone with the Wind*…she just wanted to give Gabe this one special day…he was so excited about this festival of lights thing…she didn't know how he'd managed the time to be an organizer with all the care giving he'd bestowed on her yet somehow he had managed. It was actually fun sitting here on the stern of her former homestead, *Mysts*, now that her stomach wasn't rolling over with every wave…even if she did feel like a dork with the Santa hat Gabe had bought her to keep her head warm, saying it was in tune with the spirit of the event! It was hard to believe it was almost Christmas…Advent like Lent's time of waiting was upon them…a time of forgiveness, impending new birth, rejoicing…or at least she hoped and prayed it would be…

It had been Lina's birthday this past week and she'd sent her sunflowers yet there was something just not right about being less than an hour away from her lifelong friend and not toasting the day with her. She only hoped that when all was said and done, that Lina would forgive her the miles and maybe the mistakes she'd made this past year. Soon!

"Hey, you ready for my special hot toddy?"

"Sure, bring it on…I see the lights in the distance…the parade must be getting ready to start."

"Careful, it's really hot…and I warmed the mugs with boiling water first."

Gabe squatted beside her, handed her the mug and looked deep into her eyes with a pretty damn sexy twinkle for a St. Nick wannabe, touching her fingers as he placed the mug in her hand.

"Mumm, delicious...what is this?"

"That tasty brew, m'darlin, is a drink I learned about when I was on special assignment in Minnesota one winter when Mondale was in office. It's called a Tom'n Jerry and it's batter made out of eggs and confectioners sugar...you know the real low cal, low cholesterol stuff (ha!). You mix up the batter ahead and freeze it. When the time comes for warming up, you add some boiling water, a bit of rum, a bit of brandy and a little nutmeg on the top and voila...a recipe guaranteed to bring up the body temperature and reduce the stress level. Don't worry, though, yours only has a whisper of libation. So are you warm enough?"

"And how could I not be between this concoction and all the blankets you have me cocooned within? Actually I feel like any moment I could transform myself into the butterfly I've always chased."

"Hey, just 'cause the doc has given you the all clear doesn't mean we should take chances at this stage of the game."

"What will I ever do without all your fussing and TLC?"

Kissing her atop her head, he thought, *I hope you'll never have to find out.*

Slowly the veritable parade of lights strung from mast to stern on tugs, party boats and luxury yachts of every size and sort made their way through the channel, loud with horns, and carolers, and holiday makers. There was an incredible tapestry of lights made to look like the New York City skyline in memory of 9/11, a shark with Bin Laden hanging out his mouth, reindeers riding the ropes with a red blinkin'- nosed Rudolph leading the pack. On and on they came, this parade of lights. And as beautiful as it all was, it somehow made her miss the kids who she knew would have delighted in the merriment. Tia knew she needed to hang in, though, for Gabe's sake. Again, focusing on the parade of lights instead of her dark thoughts, she thought she saw a rainbow approaching.

Standing, she said to Gabe, "Oh, look, here comes a sailboat with a rainbow." Tia thought of Helena, and though she felt happier at this moment than she had in weeks, the tears fell unbidden from her eyes, and through her tears, she saw Lina sitting on the bow, dressed in a free-flowing dress that resembled the color of a flamingo and the grace of a mermaid. In her shimmering pink outfit and matching boa draped around her neck, there Lina stood waving pom-poms and yelling, "Feliz Navidad, Tia," Beside Lina, Rod waved at Tia and Gabe, looking like a cross between Santa and King Neptune from *The Little Mermaid!!!!* Crying and laughing and hollering across the wake, Tia was beaming from inside out. Her radiant smile seemed brighter than any light on any boat or any star in any sky. Tia turned around and just stared at Gabe, who winked and whispered, "Merry Christmas, Tia."

Almost Midnight

12/22/02

Oh, what an almost year this has been… My body is exhausted, yet here I am, too wired to sleep, alone of all places in Gabe's condo. What would I do without him and without you, my laptop journal, my memory, my keeper of truths, my catharsis, conscience and mechanical friend…you take whatever I dish out, no matter how angry, afraid, confused or misguided my thoughts …so this once I want to record my hope!

Grateful is how I feel for this past year, despite being apart from my children and the ravages this disease has left on my body. I am and will be thankful for every minute. God did open a window where He/she closed a door…the cliché comes true. So when the white coats set me free early, I knew I had to give myself back to my kids for Christmas. The hard part was leaving Gabe and the cottage. True to his generous nature, he offered me this place as a safe house where I could slowly weave myself back into the lives of Sam and Meg. From all of this, I've learned and how! I'm not really that worried about Sam's acceptance; it's Meg who's going to make me earn her favor, and I guess I'd be the same way if I were her age and had the scar tissue that she's had to endure for one so young. When I called, Rory didn't seem shocked. We're meeting for coffee tomorrow to talk through some of our 'issues' as we both now realize we're much kinder and fuller people apart. Who knows, we may even become friends again some day, which would be a really good thing for the kids and for us as we've shared so much of our lives together. While I know I no longer love him as a woman, it's a gift simply not to feel so bitter about the years we spent together. Too, he'll be my barometer on how much of a shock I'll be to the kids physically, his first glance reaction being my mirror. Hopefully Lina's early

Christmas gift to me from when she was in Kemah will help...a winter white 100% cotton cap for my peach fuzz head to which she had sewn some mistletoe plant. According to Lina, the common name of the plant is derived from the ancient belief that mistletoe was propagated from bird droppings. This belief was related to the then-accepted principle that life could spring spontaneously from dung. Leave it to Lina!!! She also said that from the earliest times mistletoe has been one of the most magical, mysterious, and sacred plants of European folklore. It was considered 'a bestower of life and fertility; a protectant against poison; and an aphrodisiac.' Now that's a power plant and oh-so appropriate end to this chapter of my life. It is also just the surrogate security blanket I need to face the next couple of days, weeks, years...what am I saying, I'll be wearing this cap the rest of my life, and with luck, over lots more hair!

My energy is winding down, my hopes have never been higher. On that positive note, I'll log online and send a goodnight to Gabe...I've taped the quote my flamingo friend sent to this screen... 'when nothing is sure, everything's possible—Margaret Drabble.'